THE SISTERS OF
Straygarden Place

THE SISTERS OF
Straygarden Place

HAYLEY CHEWINS

CANDLEWICK PRESS

Copyright © 2020 by Hayley Chewins

First edition 2020

Library of Congress Catalog Card Number pending
ISBN 978-1-5362-1227-3

20 21 22 23 24 25 LBM 10 9 8 7 6 5 4 3 2 1

Printed in Melrose Park, IL, USA

This book was typeset in Berkeley Oldstyle.

Candlewick Press
99 Dover Street
Somerville, Massachusetts 02144

www.candlewick.com

This book is dedicated to my sisters.

CHAPTER

One

The house dressed Mayhap Ballastian in blue on the day her sister disappeared.

Blue for sorrow.

Blue for a bruise.

Blue for cold.

Mayhap stood in the vaulted entrance hall of Straygarden Place, peering through tiny frond-shaped windows at the silver grass that swamped them.

The grass grew taller than the house itself, surrounding it on all sides. It stuffed the keyholes and scraped against the roof. It shook the walls and made paintings shiver. It took on the color of the sky as it changed, and right now was tinted with the mysterious sort of purple that arrived every day as the afternoon faded, making the house feel more like a sunken ship than a sprawling mansion.

Mayhap tapped the heel of her shoe on the white marble floor anxiously. She straightened the cuffs of her indigo coat and adjusted her kidskin gloves.

Her droomhund sat at her ankle, whining, blinking his black, black eyes.

"Shhh, Seekatrix," she whispered, gathering him into her arms. She stroked his head. His fur was wispy as whispers and inky as a nighttime sky without stars.

"I know you're upset," she told him. "But we don't have a choice."

Mayhap and her sisters hadn't unlocked the front door since their parents had left them.

Pavonine had been only three when Cygnet and Bellwether Ballastian had gone. Mayhap had been five and could still remember her father saying goodbye—his cold hands in hers, his eyes puffy, always glancing away. Her mother had stood beside him, an elegant blur in a wide-brimmed hat. Mayhap could not remember a kiss from her, a single touch.

Hours after their departure, Winnow had discovered a letter in the lap of a porcelain doll and had read its precise instructions aloud in her best eldest-sister voice:

Do not leave the house.
Do not go into the grass.
Wait for us.

Sleep darkly.

Mayhap had asked the house to frame the letter—a single hand-scrawled page—and to hang it up above their bed as a reminder.

The rules were simple and easy to follow. Mayhap didn't like the thought of disobeying.

But now she had to.

Because she had to save Winnow.

Winnow had been missing all day. Mayhap had searched for her everywhere. And then she had seen her older sister in the silver grass. Her coat's burgundy shoulders and her dark, windswept hair. Her droomhund, Evenflee, close at her heels.

Winnow was out there.

The grass parted like curtains, allowing Mayhap to see patches of sky through the mosaic of glittering windows. Floating trees drifted through the air—a whole orchard of them—their roots as white as marzipan and as frizzy as brushed ringlets, their boughs black against the bright vermilion of their petals. Her mother had christened them *wanderroot*, and there were more in the conservatory, which Cygnet had pulled into the house with rope, blistering her hands.

Mayhap took a breath, tucked Seekatrix under one arm, and turned the key in the lock.

3

The heavy door opened easily, as though its hinge had been greased with butter. The silver strands, clinging together again, appeared as solid as a serving plate. And then a long, looping blade of grass—thick as piano wire and shiny as a sugar spoon—slithered around Mayhap's arm.

Seekatrix growled.

Mayhap shuddered. All she wanted to do was shut the door. But the door had been opened. The grass had found its way in. Dread soaked her, as though she'd climbed into a bath of icy water with all her clothes on.

"Please," she said. "I only want to find my sister—"

"You are so kind to ask us to stay," hissed the grass, drawing itself into the room.

Seekatrix yapped.

"You c-can't," Mayhap stuttered. She pushed against the grass's tendrils.

"You've opened the door, Mayhap Ballastian. An open door is an invitation. And it is not polite to retract an invitation."

"I'm sorry. I didn't mean to be impolite—"

"If we cannot be permitted to come in," said the grass, as though it were speaking with a hundred and three tongues at once, "are you going to come outside?"

Before Mayhap had a chance to answer, the grass yanked her out of the house with one swift swipe. It pummeled her, dragging her through flashing and flickering light, stinging at her cheeks, Seekatrix still in her grasp.

And then it set her down abruptly.

Mayhap's ankles rattled with the hard landing, her bones clicking like the stiff cogs of clocks. She fought to catch her breath. Coughing, she said, "I'm only looking for my sister. Winnow. I mean—have you seen her, by any chance?" Seekatrix was wriggling. She let him go, and he trotted around her dizzily.

A laugh hiccuped through the grass, and it parted its strands, then slid about her elbows and shins like snakes in paintings of gardens. "And Pavonine?" it asked. "Have you lost her, too?"

"No," said Mayhap crossly, struggling against it, "of course I haven't."

"Not yet," sneered the grass. It laughed again, and Mayhap could see up into the mauve sky, the clouds laced with the dark-orange blossoms of meandering trees. A white bat, small as a mouse, flung itself through the air, diving into dusk as though into a still pond.

"Pavonine's in the library," said Mayhap. "With

Tutto. He's telling her stories. She doesn't know Winnow's gone. I saw her—I saw Winnow—through the window. She was walking. With her droomhund. I'd searched all the rooms, and I went back to our bedroom just in case. And I saw—you *swallowed* her."

"Ah, our little liar," said the grass, tittering affectionately. It slackened its hold on Mayhap's arms and legs to brush against her cheeks.

One more laugh, she thought, *and then I'll be free.* "Why did you call me that?" she asked. "Why did you call me your little liar?"

The grass snickered, loosening around her arms and legs even more, like hair falling from a plait. "Because," it said. "Because you are ours, aren't you?"

There, thought Mayhap—there was a gap. She slipped one foot out of the silver, then the other, whipping her arms from the grass's tangle. She turned and she ran, stumbling, whistling for Seekatrix to follow.

The grass bristled, but it didn't reach for her, and Mayhap did not pause to ask why.

She ran up the wide front steps and dived into the entrance hall, Seekatrix at her heels. She threw her body against the door, turning the key in the lock as quickly as her shaking fingers would allow.

"We'll wait," said the grass. "We'll wait for you,

Mayhap Ballastian. We have been patient for a long time, and we will be patient still."

Mayhap slid to the floor. Seekatrix crept into her arms like a jittery shadow, and she let him lick away her tears. "Winnow," she sobbed into his fur. "What have you done?"

CHAPTER

Two

"She's not answering," mewled Pavonine as she banged on the door of the upstairs sitting room. Mayhap and Seekatrix stood beside her as she got down on her knees to peer through the seed-shaped keyhole. "She's locked it from the inside."

Pavonine's droomhund, Peffiandra, scratched and sniffed at the door while Seekatrix sat and twitched his ears. He knew Winnow wasn't really there.

Earlier, Mayhap had tied a black silk stocking to the doorknob on the inside of the room, letting it hang over the keyhole so Pavonine wouldn't be able to spy through it. She had locked the door and slipped the key into her pocket.

Little liar.

"I told you, Pav," Mayhap said, patting the ruched shoulder of her sister's pinafore, "Winnow is having a bad day." She felt the untrue words reverberate through her.

"But it's dinnertime," said Pavonine, getting to her feet and smoothing her skirt. She cupped her hands around her mouth and called through the mahogany door: "Winnow, it's dinnertime!" Peffiandra joined in with a howl.

Mayhap put her arm around Pavonine and led her away. "Let's go ask the house for dinner. I'm sure Winnow will be down soon."

When Pavonine finally relented, the sisters walked down the hallway together, the carpets beneath their feet as plush as tigers' pelts, their droomhunds prancing behind them. The house had lit its electric lamps, and they glowed along the walls like giant luminescent flowers, droning strange harmonies.

"She's been acting so oddly lately," sighed Pavonine. "She's always staring out the windows."

Pavonine was right. Winnow *had* been behaving uncharacteristically—for weeks now. She seemed restless as a swishing skirt. But Mayhap didn't know what to do about it. Every time she tried to ask Winnow what was wrong, her sister ignored her or changed the subject.

"She's probably missing Mamma and Pappa," said Mayhap. And she realized, with some shock, that she hadn't even been that surprised to see a glimpse of Winnow in the silver grass—as if she'd known for ages that it was exactly what her sister wanted.

"I miss Mamma and Pappa, too," said Pavonine, interrupting Mayhap's thoughts. "But I don't lock myself in rooms because of it."

"Well, you're not fourteen," said Mayhap.

"I won't do that when I'm fourteen," said Pavonine, crossing her arms and frowning stubbornly. "I swear it."

Mayhap smiled at her sister. "How about we play our guessing game, Pav?" she said. Pavonine kept her frown but nodded sheepishly. Mayhap said, "Think of an animal, think of a—"

"Got one," Pavonine replied.

"Does it have scales?" asked Mayhap.

Pavonine shook her head.

"Fur?"

Pavonine nodded.

"It's not a droomhund, is it?" teased Mayhap. "That would be far too easy."

"It's a bat," someone said behind them.

Mayhap stopped short, nearly tripping over her own buckled shoes. Seekatrix jumped up and down at her side.

"Winnow!" cried Pavonine, flinging herself into her

big sister's arms. Peffiandra ran over to lick Evenflee's face.

Winnow hugged Pavonine tightly, stroking the top of her head, but only looked at Mayhap. She didn't come any closer. She was wearing an ankle-length violet dress with a narrow skirt, embroidery running in a column down its center—a dress for a lady instead of a girl. Her hair was elegantly styled, and there wasn't a speck of dirt on her anywhere. Her shoes were clean, too. Citrine earrings dangled at her neck.

She must've asked the house to change her clothes and do her hair, thought Mayhap.

The girls could change their clothes or coiffure in a matter of moments—they only had to ask the house to see to it. But the house couldn't change Winnow's flushed cheeks, her quickened breath. She had been running. Evenflee sat panting by her side, swishing his fluffy tail. He had been running, too.

"Winnow," breathed Mayhap. "You're all right."

"Why wouldn't I be?" said Winnow. Her smile went to Pavonine.

Mayhap cleared her throat. "We were worried," she said. "Because you were in the sitting room all day— with the door locked."

Winnow only stared at Mayhap, saying nothing.

Pavonine bent down to pick Peffiandra up. She hugged the animal to her chest. Peffiandra had always been the most placid of the dogs. Her eyes relaxed sleepily. "Are you coming to dinner, Winn?" asked Pavonine, holding her cheek against Peffiandra's face.

Winnow began to answer, then paused. She looked at Mayhap with precision—with recognition—as though she had only just realized that Mayhap resembled a character from her favorite book. "Of course," she replied finally. "Of course I'm coming to dinner."

Her voice sounded as though it were echoing from another room. It sounded as dark as the coffee she'd started to drink in the mornings—the coffee Mayhap couldn't stand the smell of. It was a smell that made her feel as though she were being buried—as though her mouth were being stuffed with the damp, pungent grounds.

Mayhap coughed.

"Let's go," said Pavonine. "I'm famished."

"Yes," said Mayhap. "Let's."

Mayhap held out a hand, and Winnow came closer. She looked at Mayhap's palm as though it were an unreadable map. It took her three long seconds to entwine her fingers with Mayhap's, and when she did, her skin was icy cold.

CHAPTER

Three

Porcelain plates sat on the long dining table like lily pads, and candles glinted their light down its middle, but the air was rigid with silence.

The Ballastian sisters took their seats in high-backed chairs that curved over their heads like cresting waves. The droomhunds hopped onto stools beside them. Evenflee and Peffiandra curled up right away, lying perfectly still except for their blinking eyes, but Seekatrix squirmed and sniffled.

"Shhh, Seeka," Mayhap whispered to him.

As usual, Winnow went first. There were rules to be followed in their family, hierarchies and orders, even if their parents were gone—especially *because* their parents were gone.

"I'll have apple charlotte," Winnow said, enunciating the words.

Evenflee sneezed.

Pavonine giggled.

Mayhap said, "Pudding for dinner? You don't feel like your favorite?"

Winnow usually had a bowl of vichyssoise for dinner. That had been their mother's preferred dish. Mayhap knew she shouldn't be upset about what her sister ate, but this was yet another thing that made her feel uneasy, as though the house itself would peel away from her the way the skin is peeled off a Christmas orange.

Winnow shrugged. "I'm celebrating," she said.

"Celebrating what?" asked Pavonine, bouncing up and down in her chair.

"It's a secret."

"I love secrets," said Pavonine. "You can tell me."

Winnow looked at her plate. "Maybe I will tell you tomorrow."

Mayhap wanted this conversation to end. It made her feel weary and helpless, like an old purse with a hole in the bottom. There had been a time when she had been the keeper of Winnow's secrets, when they had both lain awake in bed after Pavonine's droomhund had put her to sleep, whispering their hopes and reveries to each other under the cover of embroidered linen. But now Winnow had begun to say, "I want to be alone. Please leave me

14

alone. Leave. Me. Alone." She said it when Mayhap suggested she play a guessing game with them, or drink tea by the fire with them, or do anything they used to do three weeks and three days ago.

Mayhap sat up straight, unfolding her napkin and placing it on her lap. "I'll have my usual dinner, please," she said defiantly. Her mouth watered at the thought of it: a steaming aubergine pie shaped like the letter *D*.

Pavonine looked at Mayhap out the side of her eye, then said, "I'll have pudding-dinner, too. Chocolate marble cake." She showed all her teeth when she smiled.

The droomhunds stayed curled up on their cushions, eyes open, waiting for bedtime. They never ate or drank a single thing. They lived off dreams alone.

Once all three sisters had asked the house for their dinner, the plates that sat on the table were topped with their requests: apple charlotte for Winnow, a golden pie for Mayhap, and a slice of chocolate marble cake for Pavonine.

Mayhap watched Winnow, who picked up her dessert spoon and prodded the apple charlotte with it.

"Why did you lock yourself in the upstairs sitting room?" asked Pavonine through a mouthful of cake. "This is delicious," she added. "We should have pudding-dinner more often."

Winnow paused, her heaped spoon raised. She looked at Mayhap, and then at Pavonine, and then at the space between them. She seemed to be balancing whether to keep with Mayhap's lie or tell Pavonine where she'd really been. She filled her mouth. "I needed to think," she said.

"What did you need to think about?" asked Pavonine.

"About Mamma and Pappa," said Winnow. "And about—" She glanced at Mayhap. "About *things*."

"Things? About the thing you're celebrating?" said Pavonine.

"I *said* I would tell you tomorrow, Pav," said Winnow. She took another quick bite of apple charlotte and stared straight ahead.

Pavonine adorned the silence that followed with a story about how Peffiandra had found a little wooden jewelry box and chewed the lid off. "I couldn't stop laughing at her," she said. "For hours." She stroked the droomhund. "You're a clown of a girl, aren't you?"

Peffiandra stared up at Pavonine with big black eyes, then went back to licking her front paws.

By the time Pavonine and Mayhap had finished their dinner, Winnow's apple charlotte was left mostly uneaten. She pushed her silver-rimmed plate away from her, sighing. "Time to sleep," she said. "Tomorrow the day will wear new shoes."

These were words Mayhap usually used to comfort Winnow when she was sad. Together, they would imagine the type of shoes the day would wear next: boots fashioned out of carmine suede, or Grecian sandals braided with ivy, or amaranth ballet slippers covered in little beaded periwinkles.

Perhaps Winnow meant them as a bridge between silence and lies. But Mayhap—full and exhausted and still shaky from her interaction with the grass—could only press her lips into a forced smile and nod.

Tomorrow, she feared, the day would be barefoot.

Dressed in lace nightgowns, the girls settled down on chaise longues in their bedroom.

Pavonine groaned. "I'm tired now," she whinged. "Why must we brush the droomhunds *every* night?" She made *every* sound like the longest word in a long history of long-haired girls.

"You know why," said Mayhap, handing Pavonine a mother-of-pearl brush with horsehair bristles.

Pavonine took the brush out of Mayhap's hand begrudgingly. "So they don't traipse the dirt of the weary world into our dreams," she grumbled.

Peffiandra seemed to consider this a summons. She jumped onto Pavonine's lap.

"Exactly," said Mayhap.

The house was spotlessly clean, but one couldn't ever be too careful with a creature one allowed to sleep in one's head.

A droomhund could press itself into the tight space of a person's mind, much like a mouse squeezing under the lip of a locked door. With the droomhunds in their minds, the blaring light that lit up behind the Ballastian sisters' eyes whenever they tried to sleep—a sensation Winnow had described to Mayhap and Pavonine in great detail after conducting what she called "an experiment"— could be muffled with the dogs' black fur. But if the droomhunds weren't brushed, the fur would prickle the insides of the girls' heads, turning their dreams sharp as hat pins and making their thoughts scatter like dropped marbles. The softer the droomhunds' fur was, the more restful the girls' sleep would be.

"But it's such a pain," moaned Pavonine. "The house does everything for us. Why can't it take care of the droomhunds, too?" She ran one hand over Peffiandra's back, the brush poised in the other.

"Because the cost of light is darkness," said Winnow. She sat opposite Pavonine, Evenflee lying beside her.

"You're always saying that," said Pavonine, her shoulders drooping. "And I don't even know what it means." She stabbed at the chaise with the handle of her brush, and Peffiandra looked up, alarmed.

"It's something Mamma used to say," said Winnow, sounding unbearably sad. "For every good thing in the

19

world, there is a little bad to go with it. The cost of having a droomhund is brushing her each night."

Mayhap tried to meet Winnow's eyes to say a silent *thank you,* but Winnow looked away.

"Why doesn't the house do it for us, though?" said Pavonine. "It does everything else."

"It doesn't *sleep* for us," said Winnow. "The dogs do that."

"I suppose," said Pavonine.

Mayhap said, "It's the way it is, Pav. Some things simply—*are.* And you can't change them." *Like the way Winnow has been acting,* she thought. She blinked back tears as Seekatrix turned a few anxious circles on her lap. Once he was lying down, she began to run the bristles of her brush through his fur.

Winnow began to brush Evenflee, too, and Pavonine—who had somehow managed to stop complaining—followed suit.

Usually, the Ballastian sisters would talk while they groomed their dogs, but tonight there were too many secrets in the air, and too many lies. The only sounds were the hush of the brushes through thick fur and the rattle of the grass against the windows.

Hush. Rattle. Hush. Rattle.

Pavonine made a quick job of brushing Peffiandra,

who endured the treatment like a rag doll. When Pavonine was done, the little dog leaped to the floor, shook as though she was wet, and scratched at the plush carpet.

"Did you do her legs?" said Winnow.

"Yes," moaned Pavonine. She rolled her eyes.

Winnow rolled hers back.

Then Pavonine began chasing Peffiandra around, squealing as the droomhund growled playfully, her fur fluffed and standing on end.

"Pav," said Mayhap. "Don't get her all excited before bed."

"Why not?" asked Pavonine, stalking behind Peffiandra, about to give her a fright. "She'll sleep when she needs to sleep."

"But you had those nightmares the last time, remember? If she can't settle down, then you won't, either. It's not just the texture of their fur that matters."

Pavonine didn't listen.

"Pavonine Ballastian," said Mayhap, "take your droomhund into the hallway right this minute. Ask the house to keep the lights off, and walk up and down slowly. She needs to be in the right state for sleeping."

Pavonine frowned, scooping Peffiandra into her arms. "Next time you want to talk to Winnow alone," she said bitterly, "just say so." She marched out of the room.

When Pavonine closed the door behind her, Mayhap looked at Winnow, who was focusing intently on brushing Evenflee's curly tail. "Winnow," Mayhap said, "why did you go walking in the grass?"

Winnow's brushing hand stopped moving. For a moment, Mayhap thought her sister was going to tell her the truth. But instead she said, "I'm tired, Mayhap."

Mayhap found a tangle in one of Seekatrix's ears and began to go over it gently with her brush, pulling it apart with her fingers. Seekatrix shook his head. "Why won't you tell me?" she whispered urgently, keeping her eyes on Seekatrix's ear. "I *saw* you, Winnow."

Winnow threw down her brush and it hit the carpet with a dull thud. Evenflee looked up, curious. "I can't sit in this house all day," she snapped. "Waiting for them. It's agonizing, not knowing anything."

Mayhap picked up the brush, which had rolled toward her. She stood, her droomhund tucked under one arm. "I can't believe you left the house, Winn. You know how dangerous it is. Mamma and Pappa—"

"Don't *talk* about Mamma and Pappa!" said Winnow, snatching the brush out of Mayhap's hand. Then she added, whispering, "Mamma and Pappa aren't here." She began to brush Evenflee again, this time more forcefully. He cringed, flinching when the bristles met his fur.

Mayhap kneeled beside Winnow's chaise, cradling Seekatrix. "Winnow, I had to *lie* to Pavonine. She would've been terrified if she'd known."

Winnow only scowled.

"It's a miracle you came back alive," said Mayhap, her voice louder now. She glanced at the windows, shuttered with silver grass.

"But I did come back," said Winnow. "I'm perfectly fine."

Mayhap looked at the carpet. She looked at Seekatrix in her arms. She looked at the door. She looked at Winnow's flushed face. "Fine," she said. It was all she could think to say.

"I just—" Winnow said. "I can't—"

Evenflee struggled, wanting to get away from her harsh brushing.

Around them, the house was quietly tidying little objects away: perfume bottles, books and pencils, stray gloves and wilted flowers. It was folding down the quilts on their bed and drawing the thick curtains so the grass couldn't watch them sleeping. The room darkened, but a fire lit itself in the grate and began to crackle, emitting a warm glow.

"You can't what?" said Mayhap.

Evenflee finally wriggled out of Winnow's arms and jumped to the floor, giving himself a good shake.

"Nothing," said Winnow. "I told you, Mayhap—I'm tired. We can talk about this in the morning." Without another word, she got into bed and climbed under the covers.

Mayhap watched, her mouth open in disbelief. The walls seemed to press nearer to her, as though they were trying to hear her breathing.

"That's enough brushing for tonight, Seeka," she said, burying her face in his sweet-smelling fur.

"Sounds about right," said Pavonine, arriving through the door with a drowsy Peffiandra in her arms.

"All right, you two," said Mayhap.

Her words echoed as though she had two mouths instead of one, and she tried not to think about the grass and the way it spoke with a hundred separate voices.

CHAPTER

Five

Mayhap, Winnow, and Pavonine lay in their crescent-shaped bed of creamy onyx, their hair spread out on embroidered pillows.

The letter their parents had left hung on the wall above their heads, framed in curlicued silver. In the black-and-white photograph that hung beside the letter, Cygnet and Bellwether Ballastian were sitting on a sofa, staring ahead seriously, their droomhunds perched on their laps.

All three girls blew a kiss to their lost parents. "Sleep darkly, Mamma and Pappa," they said in unison.

"Sleep darkly, Winnow," said Mayhap, determined not to meet her older sister's eyes. "Sleep darkly, Pavonine."

The grass made a keening sound against the windows.

The coverlet tucked itself around the girls.

"Sleep darkly, Mayhap," said Winnow, lying back and letting out a long breath. "Sleep darkly, Pavonina Carina."

"Sleep darkly, sisters," whispered Pavonine.

And then Winnow whistled for the dogs.

The three droomhunds leaped at once onto the enormous bed.

Peffiandra trotted toward Pavonine's cheek. Evenflee pawed at Winnow's collarbone. And Seekatrix bounded onto Mayhap's stomach. Mayhap rubbed his ears. He smelled of brown sugar and orange zest. He yawned, showing his black tongue and gums, the inky cave of his mouth.

Peffiandra nuzzled Pavonine's ear, then burrowed inside it like a rabbit slipping into its warren. Pavonine's breathing slowed and steadied. Her eyes fluttered closed, her eyelids like two pink petals.

Then Winnow said, "You next, Mayhap."

Seekatrix was on his back now, gnawing at Mayhap's fingers. She wished she could fall asleep with him beside her—tucked against her body or held in her arms. But that was impossible. She was a Ballastian. If she closed her eyes for too long without a droomhund inside her mind, her head would fill with a buzzing whiteness, a searing heat, like lightning burning inside her. Those were the words Winnow had used after her experiment. It made Mayhap nauseous to think of it. She rubbed Seekatrix's belly and whispered, "Come on, Seeka. Time to sleep darkly."

He sat up, tilting his head, then squeezed his way into Mayhap's mind.

The room went ashy at the edges, as though it were a singed letter, and Mayhap's thoughts turned to gauze and gossamer. Pressure sat behind her watering eyes and pinched the top of her nose as Seekatrix fussed, trying to get comfortable.

Winnow's face hovered over her, a fuzzy oval, and then Seekatrix curled up tightly and went to sleep, and everything went dark. Mayhap shut her eyes.

It was time to rest.

CHAPTER
Six

Seekatrix scrambled painfully out of Mayhap's mind, and she knew he was petrified.

Sometimes a noise would wake him, and he would flee from her head, leaving her ears ringing. But this was different. Her whole head ached and the bridge of her nose burned. Waking up had never hurt this much.

When she opened her eyes, rubbing her temples to stop the clangor in her brain, the silver ceiling came into focus above her, its ridges as defined as scars in the light of the fire.

Pavonine was still asleep. Seekatrix was sitting beside Mayhap on the bed, facing her. His growl was high-pitched, like a hummed question.

And Winnow was gone.

Mayhap clambered out of bed, and Seekatrix followed her. She asked the house for a dressing gown, and a garment as fragile as moths' wings was draped over her shoulders, pink ribbons tightening the organza around her wrists. Velvet slippers covered her feet.

When she opened the heavy damask drapes and peered through one of the thousand bedroom windows—each the size of a teacup and shaped like a nine-pointed star—she found that it was the middle of the night.

The silver grass parted its strands and swayed, revealing a navy sky dabbed with white stars. The wander-root trees hung in the air like ornate chandeliers.

As Mayhap pressed her face to the glass, the silver shrieked and scratched against the windows. She stumbled back, legs numb.

She turned to Seekatrix, her heart pounding. He was standing just behind her, still growling, and her thundering heart made her want to growl right back. "Seeka," she whispered, folding her arms. "What's going on? Why did you wake me?"

He pitched his ears forward, his growl only loudening.

Mayhap patted her thigh for him to follow her. She knocked on the intricately carved ebony screen that separated the bedroom from the bathroom. "Winnow," she said, "are you in there?"

Silence.

Mayhap asked the house to move the screen aside. The electric lamp on the wall glowed. The bathroom—a square of seamless green marble with a claw-footed tub in the middle of it—was empty.

"Winnow?" said Mayhap again. Her sister's name was peculiarly shaped in her mouth, as though it were a shard of broken china.

And Seekatrix was still growling.

Mayhap peered at the open bedroom door. She couldn't remember if it had been closed when they'd gone to sleep. She felt it call to her—pulling her as though there were an invisible wire connecting it to her heart.

"Come along," she said to Seekatrix, marching through the door. The droomhund walked at her side with his tail held halfway down, sloped like a lowered flag.

Lustring-shaded lamps lit Mayhap's way as she followed the carpet that traced the hallway's length like a gift's ribbon. The walls were dotted with mirrors of every shape and size, framed in burnished silver. As she walked, she could see other Mayhaps walking alongside her. Her dressing gown billowed like a cloak.

Four rooms down, there was another open door. Mayhap pushed past it.

And there was Winnow.

Winnow was lying in a bed shaped like a hand and carved out of oxblood marble. The curtains on the far side of the bedroom were open. The moonlight, filtered through the grass and through a thousand rose-shaped windows, brightened her face as though it had been dusted with chalk. She stirred, waking. She sat up. But Evenflee did not wriggle or slink or jump out of her mind. In fact, Evenflee was nowhere to be seen.

Mayhap stepped into the room tentatively.

"Winnow," she whispered. "Why are you in here?"

Winnow didn't answer, only rocked her head from side to side, clenching her eyes closed. Mayhap approached the bed and placed a palm against Winnow's cheek. Winnow blinked rapidly, as though she were trying to see something clearer.

Seekatrix yelped.

And Mayhap fell back from the bed with shock.

Winnow's eyes were silver, their irises eaten up by the color.

"Winnow," said Mayhap, louder now. "Winnow, what's happened? Where's Evenflee? Why were you

31

closing your eyes without him? Were you experimenting again?"

It seemed to take a few moments for Winnow to register who Mayhap was. When she did, she recoiled, her face twisted. She lay down again, turning onto her side. The sound she made could only have been described as howling.

Which was probably what woke Peffiandra and Pavonine and brought them running.

"May?" Pavonine said. She stood in the doorway in her dressing gown of petaled lace. Peffiandra sat beside her, a full stop at the end of her sentence. "May, what's going on?"

"Nothing," said Mayhap. "Go back to sleep, Pav. Everything's fine." She held a hand up to Pavonine to indicate that she should stay where she was.

But Winnow was still crying—*sobbing*. It was clear that Mayhap's words were untrue. Perhaps the grass had been right to call her a liar.

Little liar. Little liar.

Pavonine marched over to stand beside Mayhap, and Peffiandra trotted after her, darting about the room playfully.

Pavonine reached for Winnow and rubbed her arm. "Winn," she said. "It's all right. It's all right."

Winnow did not flinch at Pavonine's touch. When she opened her eyes again, Pavonine drew in a breath, but she didn't look away. Mayhap turned her face to stare at the wallpaper. On it, droomhunds flew through forests of earth-rooted trees.

"What happened to her, May?" asked Pavonine, her hand still on Winnow's arm.

"I don't know," said Mayhap. "Seekatrix woke me up, and Winnow was gone, and I found her here, and—she doesn't want me to touch her."

"I think she's hurting," said Pavonine.

Mayhap could only nod.

"Where's Evenflee?" said Pavonine.

"I don't know," said Mayhap. "I asked her, but she won't talk to me. I'm not sure she can."

As if in response to this, Winnow cried out.

"Shhh," said Pavonine, stroking Winnow's hair. "Shhh, Winn. We're going to find out what happened. I promise." She looked at Mayhap as if to say, *We promise, right?*

Mayhap frowned. Winnow was awake, which meant Evenflee had to be somewhere. If he'd left her mind after sleeping, he would normally be right next to her. "Where's Evenflee, Seeka?" she asked. But Seekatrix only stared at her.

Mayhap checked the wardrobe for Evenflee, then kneeled to peer under the bed. There was no sign of him.

"Maybe he got scared and ran away," said Pavonine. "Maybe he's hiding somewhere."

Mayhap thought about this. The droomhunds were sensitive creatures, prone to frights and shakes and shivers. Seekatrix, the most nervous of all, trembled every time he heard a door rattle.

Evenflee could have been spooked by Winnow's cries. He could have slipped under a sofa or behind a cabinet. He could be waiting for someone to find him. But when Mayhap had come into the room, Winnow looked like she was sleeping. Now she was awake, and Evenflee wasn't around. It didn't make any sense. Even if she'd been experimenting by closing her eyes without him, he would have been around. The droomhunds were always around.

"Do you think that's what's making her unwell, May?" piped up Pavonine. "The droomhunds are always with us . . ."

But Mayhap knew, behind a locked door in her heart, that whatever had gone wrong with Winnow went beyond a missing droomhund.

Their parents had told them not to leave the house,

and Winnow had, and now she was hurting and her eyes were silver, like the grass.

Winnow stirred, and Pavonine said, "May, look—"

Mayhap watched the silver of Winnow's irises seep out of her closed eyes. The color spread both upward and downward, staining her cheekbones and eyelashes.

Pavonine tucked Peffiandra under one arm and rubbed beneath Winnow's eye with her thumb. "What is it?" she asked breathlessly.

Winnow's eyes shot open. She screamed.

Mayhap took a step back. "I don't know, Pav. I don't know," she said.

"What are we going to do?" asked Pavonine. "There has to be something we can do."

Mayhap chewed on a nail. "We need to make her better," she said. "Of course that's what we have to do. We have to make her better."

"But how?" asked Pavonine. "How are we going to do that?"

She had put Peffiandra on the bed and was pressing a palm to Winnow's forehead now. Winnow was groaning. Peffiandra pawed at her.

Mayhap tried to remember what the grass had said to her the day before, but all she could remember was the feeling of being surrounded. And the word *liar*.

Pavonine spoke to the house. "Please make Winnow better," she said. "Please."

The girls waited.

Nothing happened.

A clank sounded behind them—then the squeak of a hinge.

Mayhap and Pavonine turned to see that one of the miniature windows was open, swinging back and forth. For a moment, the grass hovered beyond it. Then it began to snake its tendrils into the room, curling and susurrating, sighing and raveling. It was as if it was taunting Mayhap.

Little liar. Little liar. Little liar.

"May—" said Pavonine.

Mayhap barred her sister with her arm. "Don't go close to it. Watch that Peffiandra stays on the bed." She looked at her droomhund. "Seekatrix: stay." He obeyed.

Mayhap walked to the window and pushed the grass out of it with one hand. It clung to her, but she wrestled it back, slamming the window shut. She rubbed her skin where the grass had touched it.

"What's happening, May?" asked Pavonine again.

Mayhap could see that she was petrified.

She thought for a moment about telling her sister the truth. About Winnow going out into the grass.

36

About opening the door. But she didn't want to frighten Pavonine. She had to keep that all to herself; she had to deal with it on her own.

The only thing she could think to do was to return to the entrance hall, to ask the grass what it had done, and to hope it would answer plainly.

"I'm not sure, Pav," she said, "but we have to start somewhere. Let's look for Evenflee, all right? You can look up here and I'll go downstairs."

Pavonine nodded gravely.

Winnow moaned.

Mayhap's throat tightened, and she had to concentrate hard in order to speak. "I'll be back as soon as I've searched the downstairs rooms," she said.

But Pavonine was bending over Winnow, whispering, "Shhh, Winn, we're going to find Evenflee, and we're going to make you better," and she didn't hear her.

CHAPTER

Seven

As Mayhap wound down the carpeted stairs, someone called her name.

She jumped and looked behind her, up the curving steps, toward the room where she'd left her sisters. But the sound wasn't coming from there.

Mayhap.

Mayhap.

She gripped the marble banister. It didn't sound like the grass—cold and windy and many-throated. It didn't have Tutto's echo-metallic tone, either. It sounded like a person. But not Winnow, and not Pavonine. The voice made Mayhap's bones ache, like growing pains. It sounded like—she hoped it was, she desperately hoped it was—

It sounded like *Mamma*.

Mayhap galloped down the stairs. Maybe she would find it was nothing or maybe—maybe she would find her mother in the soft-lit drawing room, holding her arms open so that Mayhap could crawl into them. Maybe she would rest her head on her mother's shoulder. Maybe her mother would stroke her hair. Mayhap would tell her all about Winnow, and Mamma would know what to do.

She followed the voice to the conservatory. The door that separated it from the eastern wing of Straygarden Place was made of pale-blue glass. And the voice was coming from behind its warps and blurs. Seekatrix wagged his tail slowly—uncertainly—beside her.

Of course, thought Mayhap. *Of course. It makes every bit of sense.*

She let her hand hover over the doorknob.

Mayhap, said the voice again. *Mayhap, Mayhap.*

Mayhap stepped inside. The room had three walls of glass and one of brick, and crescent-shaped windows were cut into its high, transparent ceiling. The silver grass that towered all around it made the moon-windows look like *real* moons—vivid and distant. Through the glass, Mayhap could see wanderroot trees outside, floating through the night sky. Six wanderroot trees floated *inside* the conservatory, too—slow as breathing. On wrought iron tables sat pots of soil, and in the pots were dead plants. Mayhap's mother, a botanist, had been trying to figure out why nothing grew at Straygarden Place except silver grass and wanderroot trees.

The room shrieked. Or rather the *bats* in the room—the bats that lived in the branches of the wanderroot trees, the bats her father had been studying—shrieked.

They were white as milk, flying in all directions, swarming her. Mayhap drew her hands over her head.

"Mamma?" she called. "Mamma?"

"So the grass has finally got one of you," came the voice.

Mayhap's heart skipped like a stone in her chest. What an odd thing for her mother to say. The bats were flying as fast as shooting stars around her, and she couldn't see through the cloud of them.

Then the little creatures shot back up into the trees, roosting like awful, ivory-skinned fruits, and Mayhap saw Seekatrix a little way away, sitting on someone's lap, and the lap did not belong to her mother.

It belonged instead to a girl in a glistening dress.

A girl with death-white skin and streaks of silver in her blond hair.

Even her eyes were white, like boiled eggs without their shells.

Mayhap stopped.

"Mayhap," said the girl. Her voice was a misty forest. "That is your name, is it not? The house has told me all about you. The *middle* daughter." Her egg-eyes shifted in their sockets as she stroked Seekatrix's back and whispered into his ear. He arched his neck to lick her face and she let him, rubbing his fluffy head.

"Y-yes," said Mayhap. "I am the middle sister."

The girl stood and took a step toward Mayhap, holding Seekatrix. "And I am the Mysteriessa of Straygarden Place," she said.

The silver in her hair was giving Mayhap a headache.

"The—" said Mayhap, trying not to step away. "The—*who*?"

The girl smiled knowingly, the way Tutto sometimes smiled at the Ballastian sisters when they asked him a question. "I use my magic to take care of the house," she sang in a creaky voice. "I take care of you and your sisters." She kissed Seekatrix's head, and he closed his eyes with pleasure. He was so calm in her presence, not nervous at all.

"Why have I never seen you before?" asked Mayhap.

"There are things about this house you don't understand," said the Mysteriessa. She allowed Seekatrix to slip to the floor, and he ran to sit beside Mayhap. Mayhap resisted the urge to pick him up. She didn't want to be distracted.

"You called my name," said Mayhap.

"I did," said the Mysteriessa. "I hope you did not find that impertinent."

"It wasn't rude," said Mayhap. "I am only . . . confused, that's all. And worried. I'm terribly worried. It's my sister, she's—" She didn't want to cry, but she was afraid that she soon would whether she liked it or not.

The Mysteriessa approached and put a hand on Mayhap's shoulder. Mayhap felt an ache in her chest, like something missing. A keyhole without a key to put in it. "Everything is going to be all right, May," said the Mysteriessa. "I am going to help you. Do not worry about Winnow."

"You know what happened to my sister?" said Mayhap, feeling dizzy.

The Mysteriessa laughed sweetly. "Of course I do, silly. I know everything about you girls."

"I don't understand," said Mayhap.

"There, there," said the Mysteriessa. "You do

not have to understand. Not everything, anyway. You only need to listen to me, and everything will be fine. Your sister will be fine." She reached out to touch Mayhap's hair.

Mayhap closed her eyes ever so briefly and shook her head. "How did Winnow get sick?" she asked.

"You know the answer to that," said the Mysteriessa.

"She went walking in the grass."

The Mysteriessa gave a solemn nod.

"Then why haven't I fallen ill, too?" asked Mayhap. "I went looking for her."

"Winnow was out in the grass for almost an entire day. You were there for minutes."

Mayhap looked at the Mysteriessa's silver-streaked hair. "Did it hurt you, too?" she asked.

"Yes, once," said the Mysteriessa. "But I overcame it. Your sister can overcome it, too. But only if you listen to me. Otherwise—" She paused and blinked her white, white eyes. "Too much silver," she said, "and she won't survive it."

Mayhap swallowed. She was feeling increasingly exasperated with the tone of the Mysteriessa's words, the way she looked at Mayhap as though she were supposed to have answers instead of questions. "I need her to get better."

"Then you'll have to listen to me. You'll have to follow my every instruction. The first is this: do not tell Pavonine about me. It will only complicate things."

Pavonine probably wouldn't appreciate Mayhap keeping something like this from her. But she couldn't risk disobeying the Mysteriessa. Her little sister would have to understand. It was for Winnow's sake.

Mayhap swallowed hard, then answered, "All right."

"The second is this, Mayhap: you must leave Winnow to sleep. The silver will pass through her eventually. If you let her rest."

"Pass *through* her?"

"It is like any other fever," said the Mysteriessa. "It can abate."

The girls had had fevers before, and coughs, and runny noses. The house had always taken care of them, giving them broth and covering them with blankets and running steaming baths for them when they got the shivers. But the house was not doing any of that for Winnow now. It seemed as though it didn't know what to do. This was different.

"But she's not asleep," said Mayhap. "She's in pain. She's screaming, sobbing. I can't just leave her like that."

The Mysteriessa looked worried, but her voice

sounded certain. "Do not let the grass touch her again. The more she is exposed, the worse she will get."

Mayhap thought about the grass opening the window, curling through it. She shuddered. "Fine," she said.

The bats were swaying, making the branches of the wanderroot trees creak. The silver grass hugged the glass from outside, as though it were listening closely.

"Is she . . ." said Mayhap. "Are you sure she's going to be all right?"

"We can only hope and wait," said the Mysteriessa. Then she turned and began to walk away.

"Wait!" cried Mayhap. "Come back, please! I want—"

Mayhap didn't even know how to finish the sentence. She wanted to know everything. She wanted answers. She wanted the truth.

But the bats swarmed her again, and by the time she'd fended them off, the Mysteriessa of Straygarden Place was gone.

CHAPTER

Eight

A rusty scrape sounded from above.

Mayhap looked up.

One of the crescent-shaped windows in the glass ceiling was open.

The bats flew, screeching, to hide among the branches of the wanderroot trees that hovered inside the room.

And Mayhap watched, horrified, as a tangle of silver grass threaded its way into the room and around one of the bats. She gaped as the grass stole it, as it struggled and squealed, as the others cowered.

Fear leaped through her like a thousand crickets, and she ran out of the conservatory, Seekatrix grazing her calf. The grass could be doing the same upstairs— grabbing at Winnow, making her sicker.

Please be all right, she thought. *Please.*

But when she arrived at the room she had left Winnow and Pavonine in, it was empty.

The window—the one the grass had opened before, the one Mayhap knew she had closed tightly—was squeaking on its hinge again. The sound made Mayhap nauseous.

She ran up the hallway. "Pavonine!" she called.

Pavonine stepped out of one of the house's many bedrooms. Peffiandra stood beside her. "Did you find Evenflee?" Her voice was full of hope.

Mayhap tried to speak, but her tongue was so dry she couldn't form the words. "Water, please," she whispered hoarsely. A delicate glass appeared in her hand. She sipped the cold, clear liquid. "Pav," she said once she had swallowed. "Where's Winnow?"

"I left her in bed," said Pavonine.

"She's gone," said Mayhap. "She's not there anymore." She held out her empty water glass, and the house disappeared it. "I found the door open, and the window—"

"*What?*" Pavonine ran, and Peffiandra sprinted after her.

The room was as empty as Mayhap had left it. The window sang a mournful tune. Seekatrix whined along with it.

"Pav, what happened?" said Mayhap.

Pavonine was close to tears. "She was just lying

there. I thought she'd rest for a bit, and I could look around for Evenflee."

"Well, now we've lost Winnow, too," said Mayhap.

Pavonine was about to reply when there was an ear-splitting scream. It was so loud that it curled the wall-paper, as though the house were cringing and covering its ears.

Pavonine and Mayhap followed the sound of their sister's voice, their droomhunds scampering beside them. They followed it to their parents' old bedroom.

Winnow, now silent, stood on the far side of the room, at the windows, looking out at the grass with her back to the door. She didn't even notice Mayhap and Pavonine. She was holding something in her hands. In the feeble light of the lamps, Mayhap couldn't quite make out what it was.

"Winnow?" said Mayhap. "Are you feeling better? We were worried." She tried to go to her sister, but Winnow moved away, pinning herself against the wall. Mayhap held out a hand. "Winnow, did the grass come for you again? Did it touch you?"

Winnow only bared her teeth, hissing at Mayhap. Up close, Mayhap could see what she was holding: their parents' letter, taken down from their bedroom wall, still in its frame, tucked safely under glass.

Pavonine touched Mayhap's shoulder.

"Let me," she said. She turned her attention to Winnow. "Winn," she said, "what are you doing with Mamma and Pappa's letter? Did you want to read it again for comfort? I always do that when I'm not well—"

Winnow threw the frame onto the floor and stomped on it with a bare foot. The glass shattered. Blood dripped from her heel.

"Winnow!" said Pavonine. "What are you doing?"

The frame had been bent. The glass was in shards.

Mayhap crouched to pick away the broken glass, to rescue her parents' words. The note was the only thing they had left of them, not counting a few bat skeletons and some pots of lifeless soil.

Then Winnow kicked Mayhap—*hard*—her heel connecting with Mayhap's ribs. Now it was Pavonine who screamed.

Mayhap rolled onto her back, holding her side. She couldn't breathe. She could feel Seekatrix licking her face. She turned her head to see Peffiandra trembling in the corner near the door.

Pavonine dropped to her knees. "Are you all right, May?" she asked. "You're not bleeding, are you?"

Mayhap checked for blood. There was none. A little shiver went through her.

"What's happening to her?" said Pavonine in a low voice. She was looking at Winnow.

Mayhap struggled to get air into her lungs. "I don't think she knows what she's doing. It's as though she's not even here."

Winnow stooped to pick up the note. She held it between her index finger and thumb as though it were a used handkerchief. She screamed again—a loud, meaningless, cutting sound, her body curving with the effort—and tore the letter up.

"No!" said Mayhap. She lurched to her feet, hunched, her side aching, and lunged toward Winnow.

Winnow only smiled at her. Her smile was sad. No—her smile was *contemptuous*. Maybe it was both. She turned her back on Mayhap.

It was too late. The note was in pieces. They fell like rose petals to the carpet.

"Pavonine, take Winnow to our bedroom," rasped Mayhap.

Pavonine's eyes spilled out worry.

"*Now*, Pav," said Mayhap. "And listen to me—you need to stay with her. You can't leave her alone again. We don't know what she'll do." The sound of the stolen bat's squealing was still echoing in her ears. "And keep the windows closed. So she doesn't get cold."

"And you'll keep looking for Evenflee?" said Pavonine.

"I'll keep looking for Evenflee."

Pavonine nodded gravely and walked up to Winnow, and Winnow's shoulders sank. "Let's get you back to bed, Winn," she said, leading her sister out of the room. "We're going to make this all better—don't you worry."

Peffiandra followed, giving Winnow a generous berth.

For a moment, Mayhap worried that perhaps Pavonine wouldn't be safe with Winnow. But Winnow had not lashed out at Pavonine. She had turned her wrath only toward Mayhap.

She tried to comfort herself by thinking that it wasn't *really* her sister acting this way. It was the sickness. It was the silver. It was the grass. It was just as the Mysteriessa had said. But her side ached, and so did her heart. Regardless of whether she was well or not, Winnow had wanted to do her harm.

Mayhap collected the shreds of her parents' letter and read the torn words, blinking tears away. She untied the ribbon at her left wrist and slipped the pieces into her sleeve, tightening it so they wouldn't fall out. When all of this was over, she would ask the house to glue the letter together. She would ask it for a new frame.

What she really wanted to ask the house to do was turn back time—to make it so that Winnow never went walking in the grass. She wanted to ask the house to get rid of the silver grass altogether, in fact. She wanted to ask it to bring their parents back.

In the days following their parents' disappearance, Mayhap and Winnow must have asked the house a thousand times to return them. But it never did. They had realized soon enough that there were things the house could do and things that were beyond its power.

Later, when Pavonine was older and had begun to spend most of her time in the library, she explained to her sisters: "Even magic is limited. There are different types, and the type of magic determines what it can do."

And the girls had understood: The house could feed them, could clothe them, could keep its carpets clean and its mirrors shining. It could draw their baths and make their bed. It could pour them tea and serve them dinner. It could even fluff its carpets when they tripped so they wouldn't bruise their knees too badly.

But it could never give them what they wanted most in the world.

CHAPTER

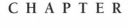

Mayhap sat in the hallway, picking little stars of glass
out of the bottoms of her slippers. Seekatrix lay on the
carpet beside her.

A few doors down, she could hear Pavonine speaking to Winnow in their bedroom, whispering comfort-
ing lies.

"You have kept the grass from her," another voice
said, and Mayhap looked up to see the Mysteriessa
standing before her. Seekatrix sat up and wagged his tail.

"She's not getting better," said Mayhap.

"You don't know that," said the Mysteriessa.

"I do. I can see. She's my sister. I know when something's wrong."

"Even our sisters can surprise us," said the girl.

"But isn't there anything else I can do?" asked
Mayhap. "To help her?"

"No. You have done all you can. You will keep doing all you can. You will leave her to rest. You will not agitate her any longer."

This reminded Mayhap of Winnow's words to her. *Leave me alone. Leave. Me. Alone.*

Mayhap laughed bitterly. "Why should I trust you?" she said. "I don't know you. I don't know who you are. I don't care if there are things I don't understand about the house; you need to explain it to me if I'm going to—"

"Can I sit beside you?" asked the Mysteriessa. The words had cracks in them, like dropped and mended vases.

Mayhap didn't exactly want the Mysteriessa to sit beside her, but she didn't see how she could say no, either. So she nodded silently—and couldn't help but squirm when the Mysteriessa's arm brushed against hers. Her skin was cold, like a china doll's.

The Mysteriessa leaned toward Mayhap and whispered, "I've been here a long, long time." She looked down the hallway and back at Mayhap. "I'm the one who made this place what it is. Before, it was only an ordinary house."

Mayhap sat up straighter. "You made the grass?" she said.

The Mysteriessa shook her head. "No, no. Not the grass. The grass was here before everything."

Mayhap looked down at her folded arms. "How many years have you been the Mysteriessa?"

"One hundred and twelve."

"So you've looked after many families before us."

"I've taken care of all of them." The Mysteriessa smiled. "I told you. I understand how things work around here. That is why you must trust me, Mayhap."

Mayhap didn't want to rely on the Mysteriessa. But she needed help. She had so many questions. "The other families who lived here before us," she said. "Their portraits are in the gallery. Did the grass ever make *them* sick?"

"Sometimes. But most of them didn't stay long enough. Most of them couldn't last."

"Why not?" asked Mayhap. "Please," she implored. "Tell me."

The Mysteriessa blew out a sigh. "Fine," she said. "But only if you promise not to tell Pavonine. We don't have to make this any more complicated than it already is."

Mayhap's stomach tingled, but she said, "I promise," and she shifted so that she was facing the Mysteriessa. Seekatrix curled up on her lap.

"The grass takes things," said the Mysteriessa. "From families. So that they can live here."

"*Takes* things?"

"It's so that the house can look after them," continued the Mysteriessa. "So that the magic of the house can touch them. It's the cost of it."

The Mysteriessa paused as though she were remembering.

"Once," she said, "a man came to the gate. The house had been standing empty for years, so the grass offered it to him. The man accepted the house gladly, even after the grass told him that he would have to give something up. When he stepped inside, he couldn't believe its grandeur. He had a nice hot bath, and after a sumptuous dinner of roast lamb and figs, he fell asleep in one of the house's large, clean beds.

"The next morning, the house served him a delicious breakfast of rich coffee and tea cakes—but he could not eat a single bite or swallow a single sip. The tea cakes tasted like mud; the coffee, like water from a dirty puddle. I told him to leave, but he wanted the house. He was stubborn. He had never seen a place so beautiful.

"The house kept serving the man food—rich, lavish meals—but he could not stomach any of it. The grass had taken good tastes from him. *Taken* them, as though they were coins in a purse.

"Eventually, after weeks of being able to eat only the most meager of mouthfuls, he crawled out into the silver grass. But he was so weak that he died before he could get to the gate. If he'd only listened to me, he might have survived.

"That's what I do, Mayhap. I help the families who live here. I help them to enjoy the luxury of the house but also to manage the grass's magic. Because if they don't, tragedy befalls them."

The story sifted through Mayhap like flour through a sieve. She hugged Seekatrix tightly. "What other sorts of things does the house take?" she asked.

"Oh, sometimes it's memory, sometimes music. Sometimes it's love, or language, or solitude. The cost of light is darkness."

"Our parents used to say that," said Mayhap.

"That does not surprise me. It is the motto of Straygarden Place."

"Is this—is Winnow's sickness—is it one of the things the grass takes? Her health? Or—is that why our parents left? Did it take *them*?"

The Mysteriessa shook her head quickly. "No," she said. "It's like I said: Winnow's sickness is a consequence of touching the grass, of being out there for so long. And I—I don't know why your parents left. I'm sorry, Mayhap. I did try to get them to stay. But they insisted."

"You *knew* them?" asked Mayhap, identifying the tight, vicious feeling in her chest as jealousy.

The Mysteriessa nodded. "For a little while, yes."

Then it dawned on Mayhap. "The grass took *sleep* from us," she said. "That's why we have droomhunds. That's why we can't close our eyes for more than a minute—"

"Yes," said the Mysteriessa. "You're right. And I was the one who interceded on your behalf. I brought the droomhunds to your beds. So you could get your rest."

"So you only appear when something goes wrong?"

"When there's a conflict between the grass and the family, yes."

"None of this makes any sense," snarled Mayhap. "None of it." The ideas were a jumble of knotted ribbons in her mind, and she couldn't separate them out.

The Mysteriessa looked at the carpet. "I'm sorry, Mayhap."

Mayhap buried her face in Seekatrix's fur. Her helplessness made her furious, the kind of anger that came after you touched a hot stove. "Don't be sorry," she said to the Mysteriessa. "Be *helpful*."

"But I *am* sorry, Mayhap," said the Mysteriessa. "Just keep the grass from touching Winnow and let her rest, and it'll all be well. I'm sure of that." She touched Mayhap's shoulder, but Mayhap shrugged her hand away. Seekatrix whined softly.

"Just leave me alone," Mayhap said.

She felt the Mysteriessa drifting from her like a dissipating mist.

"What are we going to do, Seeka?" she moaned. "What are we going to do?" She looked down the hallway, toward the room she shared with Pavonine and Winnow.

She heard Pavonine's faint voice again. "Would you like me to tell you a story, Winn?"

"A story," Mayhap said to Seekatrix, and his ears darted forward.

She stood and began to walk, and her droomhund followed her dutifully.

Mayhap had never liked the library.

Though Pavonine often spent entire days there—reading stories herself and asking Tutto to tell them to her—Mayhap had visited it just a handful of times.

She went there only when Pavonine begged her to go—usually on Tutto's birthday or when Pavonine wanted to show her something in a book from the reference section: an encyclopaedic entry on some outlandish animal, or the pressed and preserved leaf of a rare and irreplaceable plant.

The truth was, Mayhap hated the library. She hated it because the books, lined up like an army, made her feel as though there was so much she didn't know about the world and about herself.

And she hated it because it always—*always*—smelled of coffee.

Her parents had asked for a coffee trolley to be added to the room, and there it remained. According to Tutto, they'd said that the smell of coffee was a bewitching thing, able to make anyone think faster and think better. Mayhap liked the *idea* of coffee— and the image of her mother and father bent over their books, cups of the steaming elixir by their sides—but the smell was nearly unbearable. It made her feel as though someone were burying her. She could taste earth on her tongue, could feel the weight of soil on her chest. It made her want to cough and cough until she spat up blood.

Which is to say: going to the library was no small feat.

But she would do it for Winnow.

The library had a floor of green marble. Sofas were dotted around it, as well as reading desks with low-bent lamps. Shelves lined the walls and reached all the way up to the domed ceiling, curving with it, the books somehow staying on their shelves even as they met the oculus in the cupola's center.

In the middle of this large circular room was the coffee trolley, positioned between two velvet armchairs. Tutto stood beside it.

Tutto was a large hippopotamus—about the same size as a *real* hippopotamus, Mayhap guessed—fashioned out of silver and holding all the library's thousands and thousands of catalog cards. He had about a hundred palm-sized drawers in his left side, and he moved about on creaky wheels. Each of the drawers contained countless cards, and each card was inscribed with the name of a library book.

Winnow seemed to remember a time when Tutto had not been alive—when he was unable to speak. She had told Mayhap and Pavonine about climbing onto his back, feeling the hammered metal beneath her hands. But she couldn't remember how he'd started talking. She used to say that maybe he got tired of sitting in a room filled with words while not having anything to say himself. Mayhap couldn't remember a time before he'd spoken, and neither could Pavonine.

Now, as she and Seekatrix approached him, she unblocked her nose and tried not to wince. "Hello, Tutto," she said. Seekatrix barked once, as if to say hi.

The great hippopotamus turned around on his wheels, his drawers rattling and tinkling. "Ah!" he said. "Mayhap! Good early morning to you. And dear old Seekatrix. I was just asking the house for a cup of coffee. I do love the smell."

Mayhap nodded. "That's nice," she said. Seekatrix wagged his tail and trotted in a circle gleefully.

"Oh, I'm sorry, Mayhap," said Tutto. "Of course, of course. You don't like the smell and that is why you don't come to the library, isn't it? Let's wheel away from the trolley, then, no harm done. One shouldn't let something as petty as a smell keep one from the library. A library is a place where dreams are categorized. Isn't that a wonderful idea? For all we know, we are caught in the mind of an artist, and each of these books is a dream she has had."

Mayhap thought that was a pleasant enough idea, but she had other pressing concerns. She did appreciate, however, how kind Tutto was to her even though she hadn't paid him a visit in so long.

"It must be something special that's brought you here," said Tutto, "since Pavonine isn't with you, and it is not my birthday." He stopped. "It's not my birthday, is it?"

Mayhap almost allowed herself to laugh. But then she remembered Winnow's cries, and all the laughter in her was frozen in place. "No," she said. "It's not your birthday. I came to check if you had any books about the grass—or about the families who lived here before."

"Oh?" Tutto's eyes widened with concern. "And why would you need books like that?"

"Winnow's ill," Mayhap said, "and I don't know what to do. And Pavonine always says every answer under the moon and stars can be found in the library."

"Hmmm," said Tutto. "I do hope Winnow gets better soon. What ails her?"

"We don't know," said Mayhap, lying a little. "We think—*I* think—the grass has made her sick. But we don't know exactly. That's why I thought if I found some books . . . I want to see if anyone else who lived here—if anyone else has gotten sick."

Tutto looked at Mayhap quizzically, narrowing his eyes. "That's terrible to hear, Mayhap. Winnow has been coming to this library since she was four years old. I do hope she gets better." He looked at the walls, as if wanting to see through them and scowl at the grass, then wheeled around to face Mayhap again. "Now, you know how this works, don't you? You haven't forgotten?"

Mayhap nodded. "I haven't forgotten."

Tutto spun around on his wheels, his drawers facing Mayhap.

Mayhap cleared her throat so that she could enunciate her request clearly. "I'm looking for books about the silver grass that surrounds Straygarden Place," she said. She clasped her hands together and waited.

From inside Tutto's cavernous body, she could hear

a ruffling and a rattling, like pages being turned very quickly in a book and spoons clattering onto tables. Then a rumbling sound echoed. The rumbling went on and on, and Mayhap thought it would never end. When it finally stopped, the little drawers remained closed. Not one opened, and no catalog card was presented to her. Mayhap huffed.

"That means," said Tutto, "that there are no books in this library that have anything in them about the grass."

"How can that be possible?" Mayhap said, half to herself and half to Tutto. She looked around the sweeping library. There must have been thousands of books in it.

Tutto had swiveled to face her again. "It isn't too surprising," he said, "when you consider that this house is a rather lonely one."

"Mamma and Pappa—they wanted to. Write about it, I mean. But they left. They left us. They never got the chance."

"There, there," said Tutto, nudging her with his warm metal nose. "We still have to address the matter of the families—the ones who used to live at Straygarden Place."

Mayhap nodded, gritting her teeth. Coming to the library had been a pointless pain. There probably wouldn't be any books about the other families, either. And then what would she do?

Tutto seemed to read her mind. "There's nothing for it but to try, Mayhap." He spun around so that the drawers in his left side faced her again.

Mayhap aligned herself with Tutto's drawers. And maybe it was the coffee smell, or maybe it was feeling verklempt over Tutto's gentleness, or maybe it was everything that was going on with Winnow, but instead of saying, "I'm looking for books about the families who have lived at Straygarden Place," she found herself saying, "I'm looking for books about my family."

She realized too late; the process had already begun.

The rattle again, then the rumble. But this time, after a few seconds, one of Tutto's drawers shot out like an extended arm, and a card flew from it, tumbling through the air toward Mayhap, twisting like a diving bat.

She jumped to snatch at it.

At first, the letters skittered like ants. But then her vision settled, and the card settled, and she could read it clearly: *The Collected Diaries of Quiverity Edevane.*

"I don't understand," she said under her breath.

Seekatrix growled.

"Let me help you there, Mayhap," said Tutto, and he wheeled about to stand beside her, careful not to bump her over. He read the card. "Oh, dear," he said. "No, no. That's not right." The drawer in his side shot open, and the card was drawn back into it.

"What happened?" asked Mayhap, her heart turned spiky.

"Oh, it's only a mix-up," said Tutto. "You asked for information on your family, and I'm afraid the wrong card was brought up."

Mayhap hesitated. "But—Tutto, *you* chose the card."

"See, that's where you're wrong. The library chose it. It's an arcane process, even to me. Anyway, let's try again. Nothing more for it than to try again. I daresay even magical libraries can have glitches."

"But why would the house bring up a card with the name Quiverity Edevane on it when I asked about my family?"

"It is strange," said Tutto. "Clearly you are *not* an Edevane. Why, you're a Ballastian, through and through. Eyes like dug holes, that's what your mother used to say. And skin like a peach rose. A botanist's daughter, through and through."

Something tickled in Mayhap's throat. The coffee smell made her skin itch. She couldn't help but feel that the erroneous card was some sort of garbled message.

If only she could figure out what the message was. "I don't understand," she said. "I don't understand anything."

"Now, that's not true." The kindness in Tutto's eyes burned, making Mayhap want to cry. "There are plenty of things you understand. Now, we need to find a book that can help Winnow. Does that sound like a good idea to you?"

Mayhap gave a single nod. "I—I am looking for books about the families that have previously lived at Straygarden Place. Please."

Tutto's insides grumbled—again. One of this drawers was flung out—again. Another card pirouetted into the air, somersaulting to land in Mayhap's palm. Tutto looked over her shoulder as Mayhap read the words aloud: "*The Book of Records: Details Concerning the Residents and Ex-Residents of Straygarden Place.*"

"Ah, you see," said Tutto. "This time you have received the correct card."

Seekatrix barked happily.

Mayhap was relieved, but she couldn't stop thinking about the previous card. She stared at the new card in her hand.

"Aren't you going to ask for it, then?" said Tutto.

"Yes," said Mayhap. "Yes, of course. Could I please

take a look at"—she consulted the card, careful to get the words exactly right—"*The Book of Records: Details Concerning the Residents and Ex-Residents of Straygarden Place.*"

Tutto and Mayhap both scanned the library's shelves.

Then Mayhap caught sight of a large book taking its time to wriggle out of a shelf, as though it had been jammed in too tightly. As soon as it freed itself, it flew through the air, descending toward her.

Mayhap's knees buckled when she caught it. Its cover was shiny—a deep scarlet with gilded lettering.

"Might be best to put it down and flip through it carefully," said Tutto.

Mayhap carried the thick book over to one of the reading tables. Tutto squeaked on his wheels behind her, and Seekatrix scratched at her leg when she sat down, wanting attention. "Shhh," she told him, patting his head.

The pages were as thin as sheaves of voile. Each one was divided into columns: *Name, Lost Quality, Date of Arrival, Date of Departure,* and *Notes.*

Mayhap read out the words in the *Lost Quality* column, struggling to pronounce them because the smell of coffee had lodged itself deep in her lungs. *"Language.*

All sweet smells. Silence. Mornings. Harmonious music. Decision-making."

Tutto read over her shoulder: *"Hellos and goodbyes. Good tastes. Imagining. Color.*"

"*Good tastes,*" repeated Mayhap. The name of the man who had lost good tastes was Algernonian Greft, and under the notes section there was one word: *Deceased.* Mayhap twitched. This was the man the Mysteriessa had told her about.

"Go to the end of it," said Mayhap. Her blood had turned to coffee, and it was pumping through her. She was drowning in the smell of it.

Tutto flipped to the back of the book with his nose to read the last entry. *"Ballastian, Cygnet and Bellwether. Daughters: Winnow, Mayhap, and Pavonine.*" His gaze lingered on the column labeled *Lost Quality.* "*Sleep,*" he read.

"There's a note next to it," said Mayhap. "*Residents given droomhunds to cope. It's just what she said.*"

"Just what who said?" asked Tutto.

"Oh, no one."

She scanned a few more pages. As far as she could see, no other family was given anything in order to cope.

Tutto used his snout to page through the book quickly. "This is fascinating! Mayhap, *hundreds* of families lived here before you and your sisters. The durations of their stays were short. Look—this one is three weeks. And this one is two days." He paused, looking at her thoughtfully. "If you'd had to give up sleep altogether, you probably also would have left after a few days. But your family has been here ten years. Because of the droomhunds." Both Tutto and Mayhap angled to look at Seekatrix, who had been sitting beside Mayhap's chair quietly. "No wonder," he snorted, "those other families didn't do much writing about the grass—or anything else."

Mayhap had to tell Pavonine about this. She had to tell her about the Mysteriessa.

Winnow's sickness was like a puzzle she couldn't complete, but she felt sure that if she and Pavonine put their heads together, they could solve it.

"Can I show this book to Pavonine?" she asked Tutto.

The hippopotamus's eyes brightened. "Certainly you can," he said, "if you bring her here."

"But—can't I take—"

"This is a reference book, Mayhap," said Tutto. "You are not permitted to remove it from the library. That's why we have so many cozy chairs here."

"Of course," said Mayhap. She should have remembered that. "I'll bring Pavonine here instead."

But *of course* was right—*of course* she couldn't do that.

They could not leave Winnow alone, and they could not risk triggering another one of her episodes by trying to move her.

"I'm afraid it's coffee time," said Tutto. He began to wheel away.

"Tutto," said Mayhap. "Couldn't you make an exception? Just for this one book?"

Tutto frowned. He opened his mouth as though he were about to acquiesce, then shook his head rapidly. "No, no," he said as though scolding himself. "It won't work."

"What won't work?" said Mayhap. "It's your library. Surely you make the rules."

Tutto shook his head emphatically again. "No, Mayhap. The library belongs to the house. And the house has rules. And the rules will be followed."

Silence sat between them like a looming wall before Tutto spoke. "I'm going to get back to my coffee. I hope you don't mind."

Coffee. Mayhap really needed to get out of the library. "No, of course not, Tutto," she said. "Goodbye. Thank you for your help."

CHAPTER

Eleven

It was not easy stealing *The Book of Records* from the library.

Getting it out of the room was simple enough, especially since Tutto was standing over one of the reading desks with his eyes closed, lapping steaming coffee out of a porcelain cup. But as Mayhap walked toward the bedroom she shared with her sisters, the tome grew heavier and heavier in her arms.

When she eventually reached the landing at the top of the stairs, she was sweating and her arms were aching, and the book was so heavy that she had to push it along the floor while Seekatrix growled at it unhelpfully. After a while, she gave up and stood in the hallway and called Pavonine's name. She couldn't push the book any longer.

By the time Pavonine appeared, Peffiandra prancing beside her, Mayhap was splayed out on the carpet. Her legs felt about as sturdy as chocolate mousse.

"Did you find him?" asked Pavonine. She looked around for Evenflee. When she didn't see him, she sighed with disappointment. Then she spotted the book. "What's that?" She raised an eyebrow.

"I went to the library," said Mayhap. "I need to show you something." She sat up, wheezing.

Pavonine crossed her arms. "What's wrong with you?" she asked. "Are you sick, too?" The fear in her eyes sparked like a faulty bulb.

"No, I'm fine. It's just that the book kept getting heavier," said Mayhap.

"Heavier?"

"Try to lift it," said Mayhap. She motioned to *The Book of Records*.

Pavonine did. And couldn't. "Mayhap, what *is* this?" she said.

"I went to the library to look up books about the grass. There weren't any, but I did find a record of all the families who have lived at Straygarden Place." Mayhap struggled to push the heavy thing toward Pavonine. "Look," she said.

74

Pavonine sat on the carpet and opened the book. She stared at the pages. Then she stood up and put her hands on her hips. "Mayhap, I thought you were going to search for Evenflee."

"I know, Pav, but just—"

"What am I supposed to be seeing, exactly?"

Mayhap scrambled toward the book. The pages had *disappeared*. In their place sat a hunk of solid white marble.

"There were *pages* in it a few minutes ago," she said desperately. "With words on them. Columns." She ran her hand over the stone. It was smooth and cold.

Pavonine squinched her face up. "May, you said you were going to look for Evenflee."

"Pav, there were words in here—"

"So you're saying the book turned to marble?" asked Pavonine.

"I was trying to help, Pav. This is important. I know it is." Mayhap gritted her teeth. "I don't know how it turned to marble—or *why*—but it was a book before."

"I don't think books are going to help us with this," said Pavonine. "Or Tutto, or anyone. Even the house doesn't know what to do."

"But the grass, Pav. It takes things from people. You

can only stay here if you give something up. Some people gave up"—Mayhap put her hands to her temples—"what were they again? Good tastes. Solitude."

"Solitude? I don't know what you're talking about, May."

"Why do you think we can't sleep?"

"It's a thing our family has, like brown eyes and dark hair."

"But what if I told you it *wasn't* something we were born with? That the grass *stole* sleep from us?"

"I would say that doesn't sound like it has anything to do with Winnow being sick."

Pavonine sat down again, beside Mayhap. She put her hand on Mayhap's hand. "We should focus on looking after Winn," said Pavonine. "On finding Evenflee—"

"She won't let me near her, Pav," said Mayhap. "And Evenflee is gone. I haven't seen him anywhere. For all we know, the grass could have taken him."

"Don't say that!"

"But it could be true!"

"We don't know that. We don't know that yet. We have to keep trying."

Mayhap pulled her hand away from Pavonine's. "Maybe you *like* that she hates me. That *you* get to look after her. You get to have her all to yourself."

Pavonine looked hurt. She stood up and walked away. Distantly, a door clicked closed.

Mayhap kicked the marble book. Her big toe stung. She rubbed her eyes and resisted the urge to scream into the carpet.

"That's what happens when you remove a reference book from the library," said a voice. "It's one of the house's rules."

Mayhap had goosebumps all the way up her neck as she turned around to face the Mysteriessa.

The girl looked smaller—or maybe Mayhap was only seeing her clearer. Her eyes were as white and waterless as pebbles.

"I wasn't going to tell her about you—I promise," said Mayhap. "I only wanted her to know about the grass. About it taking things. I thought it might help—"

"I've told you, Mayhap," said the Mysteriessa, her voice edging toward impatience. "The only thing you can do is keep Winnow away from the grass and let her rest."

"Please," said Mayhap. "Tell me something that will actually *help*. Tell me how to—"

"I have already told you, Mayhap."

"No," said Mayhap. "No." She stood and moved toward the Mysteriessa. The girl stepped back, as though she were afraid. "Tell me your name," said Mayhap. "At least tell me your actual name. How am I supposed to believe a word you're saying?"

"You're to believe me, Mayhap, because I have lived here for all your life, for all my life, and for all the lives of those who have come and gone." The Mysteriessa looked at the rectangle of marble that had once been *The Book of Records*. "Now, I'll take that," she said. She lifted it as though it were as light as a folded cardigan and began to walk away.

Mayhap watched her get smaller and smaller.

Down the hall, she could hear Winnow crying.

She covered her ears. "Please," she said. "Tell me what to do." She didn't know if she was talking to herself, to Seekatrix, or to the house. Her whispered words sounded like wind in her ears.

She curled up on the mulberry carpet, and it grew thicker around her.

Maybe she only needed to sleep darkly for a little while. Maybe she would feel better then. But she was too frightened—too *upset*.

Seekatrix licked her face.

"I love you, Seeka," said Mayhap, holding him close. The droomhund wriggled, and Mayhap's sleeve rustled. She sat up and undid the ribbon that tightened it around her wrist. Her parents' note, in all its ripped shreds, fell out.

Mayhap spread the pieces out on the carpet, arranging them so that she could read the note. It had always comforted her that the words on this piece of paper— now *pieces* of paper—had been inked by one of her parents' hands. But she found it too painful to look at the words now. She flipped the torn pieces over.

That's when she noticed the *other* words.

They were stamped on the back in pale-blue ink.

All contractual disputes should be referred to the Office of Residents' Concerns.

She looked down the long hallway.

The house was under no obligation to respond— but she could try.

"Um," she said, "could you please direct me to the, um, Office of Residents' Concerns?"

Mayhap sat in silence, Seekatrix blinking on her lap.

And then the carpet began to move.

CHAPTER

Twelve

The carpet, it seemed, knew the way to the Office of Residents' Concerns.

Mayhap sat, petrified, clutching Seekatrix, as it drew her along the hallway. It undulated and slid. It jostled and skidded. Her stomach flipped, and she closed her eyes, but not for too long—not so long that she would see that burning whiteness behind her eyelids that was every Ballastian's curse.

The carpet bore Mayhap to a door that was as black and shiny as Italian vinegar. It had a silver plaque on it. The plaque said: OFFICE OF RESIDENTS' CONCERNS.

The carpet bucked like a pony, nudging Mayhap to her feet, then once again became an unmoving softness beneath her slippers.

Seekatrix wriggled to get free. She put him down, and he stood beside her, staring at the door.

Mayhap prided herself on knowing every inch of Straygarden Place—every corner and crook, every window and whisper—and yet she had never seen this door. It didn't look like any of the other doors in the house, either, which were all smoothly varnished mahogany.

Seekatrix growled in a strange, scared way—the same way he had growled when he'd woken her up. Her heart blattered in her chest, but she took a deep breath and opened the door with a click.

The Office of Residents' Concerns was neatly ordered. It was a square room with wallpapered walls. A desk sat against the grass-swamped windows. Two armchairs had been placed in front of it. The armchairs were covered in haircloth as wiry as a droomhund's eyelashes.

Mayhap sat down in one of them, and Seekatrix jumped nimbly onto her lap.

The desk, up until this point, had been clear. But when Mayhap sat down, a wad of papers appeared before her. The stack was tied with a black grosgrain ribbon. Mayhap sat forward, watching as the ribbon untied itself. She moved closer to try to read the words on the uppermost sheet of paper—but there were none. It was blank as a cloud.

Mayhap took the pages in her hands and flipped through them. On the last page, her parents' names were printed. Their signatures hung above the letters like squashed insects.

"Mamma and Pappa," said Mayhap to Seekatrix. "They signed this. But all the other pages are blank."

The desk quavered on its feet as though in disagreement. The pages sifted out of her hands.

"Wait," said Mayhap. She tried to grasp them, but the edges nicked her skin, and she let go, rubbing at the paper cuts they left behind.

She watched as the pages moved apart, spreading out on the desk, turning to images. *Moving* images— pale colors with swabs of black and gray and silver.

She watched as her parents, Cygnet and Bellwether Ballastian, arrived at a gate—an enormous wrought iron gate with the words STRAYGARDEN PLACE worked into it. She watched as her mother soothed the baby in her arms—Pavonine, it must have been Pavonine— and as two small girls played on the path behind her.

That's me, Mayhap thought. *And Winnow.*

Her mother's face lit up like a lamp when she caught

a glimpse of the floating wanderroot trees through the silver grass. "Look, Bell," she said. "There they are."

Bellwether gasped at the bats dancing over their heads.

Her parents seemed to be waiting for something. They shuffled their feet on the cobbles.

Pavonine was sleeping peacefully in her mother's arms—her face a pink rose—and the silver grass, tall as the sky, swayed beyond the iron spires of the gate. Her mother could've touched the grass with her fingertips if she'd reached through the gate. But she didn't.

Mayhap wanted to say *Don't go inside; don't do it.*

But she couldn't speak to her parents, or to her sisters, or to her past self. She could only observe.

They all looked strange without their droomhunds at their sides, as though they were missing their shadows.

And then something was moving through the grass. Something was coming toward them. Some*one*. A girl.

The Mysteriessa.

Seekatrix cried on Mayhap's lap as she leaned closer to the desk, wanting to see everything—every detail.

The Mysteriessa, walking up to the gate, her dress like metallic rain, her eyes as white as fresh snow.

"What brings you to Straygarden Place?" she asked Mayhap's parents.

It was Mayhap's mother who spoke. "My name is Cygnet Ballastian," she said, "and this is my husband, Bellwether. And our daughters: Winnow, Mayhap, and Pavonine."

"Tell me why you are here," said the Mysteriessa.

"I'm a botanist," said Cygnet. She peered through the iron gate at the silver grass. "I've heard about the incredible plant life you have here. I don't think there's anything like it in the world." She straightened, bouncing a fussing Pavonine in her arms, and then handed the baby to Bellwether, who took her and tapped her nose with the tip of his finger. "I want to study the grass— and the trees," said Cygnet, turning back toward the Mysteriessa.

"You want to prove something," the Mysteriessa said, as though the fact were written plainly on Cygnet's forehead.

Cygnet stared right back. "Yes," she said, "I do."

Mayhap shuddered. The Mysteriessa had a talent for knowing what other people wanted, deep down. But what did *she* want herself? Mayhap couldn't tell.

The contract showed the wind ringing through the grass's stiff strands.

Mayhap's mother said, "My husband studies bats.

He's a chiropterologist. A zoologist, really, but he specializes in bats." Her words were questions, rising notes. A crescendo was coming. "When we learned of this place, it sounded as though it had been . . . *made* for us."

Mayhap's father now stepped forward. "The Academy hasn't taken kindly to our hypotheses about magic and the natural world. If we could work from here, if we could conduct experiments—" Desperation pinched his vocal cords.

"Yes," said the Mysteriessa, "I understand." She looked from Cygnet to Bellwether to Pavonine, then let her eyes fall to where Mayhap and Winnow were standing in their white shoes and stockings, a little way behind their parents.

And with that, she opened the gate, and she let the family in.

The images began to move more quickly: Cygnet, stepping through the gate with Bellwether behind her, Mayhap and Winnow following. The Mysteriessa leading them to the house, the grass moving out of the way. The door closing behind all of them. Her family inside the considerate house, the silver grass pressing against the windows in the enormous entrance hall.

Then the piece of paper blurred like running watercolors, and the picture dissolved.

Another scene formed: the Office of Residents' Concerns. It looked exactly like it did now. Mayhap's mother sat in one chair, and her father sat in the other. Mayhap and Winnow played a clapping game on the rug, chanting softly. Pavonine was still in Bellwether's arms. The Mysteriessa pointed to a pile of papers that appeared on the desk, the words upon the pages scrawled in black swooping ink. Bellwether riffled through the contract, balancing Pavonine, who was tucked into the crook of his elbow.

"What will we have to give up?" asked Cygnet.

"You don't get to choose," said the Mysteriessa. "It's not like going into a sweet shop. Once you've signed the contract, something will be taken from you. *I* will choose."

Mayhap's mother looked wistfully out the windows as a wanderroot tree drifted past. "We've come this far," she said. "We have to stay. We have to sign it. Bell?"

Mayhap's father smiled, but he was frowning at the same time.

Cygnet touched his hand. "Everything is going to be fine, Bell." She looked over at Mayhap and Winnow. "We're doing this for them," she whispered. "Right?"

The Mysteriessa said, "Have you made up your minds?"

Hope filled Cygnet's and Bellwether's eyes. Hope that she wouldn't take too much from them.

A pen appeared on the desk, and Mayhap's mother took it in her hand. She printed her name, signed the contract, and slid it over to Mayhap's father, who did the same. Cygnet cooed at Pavonine.

And then the Mysteriessa said, "Congratulations. You are now the proud owners of Straygarden Place. The house will look after your every material need." A pause sounded through the office. "And," she added, "you will never sleep again."

The paper in front of Mayhap became littered with unreadable, rain-soaked images.

Mayhap sat in the chair, shaking, stroking Seekatrix's back. "Seeka," she whispered. "The grass isn't the one who takes things from the families who live here. It's the Mysteriessa." Seekatrix pushed his nose under her elbow, as though wanting to hide. "If the grass isn't the one who took sleep from us, Seeka, then maybe the grass isn't the one making Winnow sick. Maybe it's *her*."

Mayhap dragged the chair closer to the desk. "I want to ask a question," she said.

A pen and a fresh piece of paper appeared before her.

She scribbled seven words: *Why did the Mysteriessa give us droomhunds?*

The pages of the contract swirled.

They showed the Mysteriessa standing in the silver grass at night. She whistled a tune, a song of four notes, and five droomhunds came bounding toward her. They were small as kittens. The Mysteriessa gathered the bundles of fur into her arms—black as night and squirmy as earthworms. She carried them to the girls' nursery, where baby Pavonine was bawling, red-faced, and toddler Mayhap was lying in bed, rubbing her scratchy eyes, and small Winnow was curled up, feverish. Their parents were stooped over Pavonine's cot, their skin as ashy as cold fireplaces. They obviously hadn't slept since they'd arrived at the house, and neither had Mayhap and her sisters. The Mysteriessa placed a little black ball of furry darkness—a droomhund—into each of the girls' beds and then gave one to Cygnet and one to Bellwether.

"But *why*?" breathed Mayhap. "I want to know why."

The contract shivered as though bristling. *Be patient,* it seemed to say.

It showed the Mysteriessa watching from the door as the droomhunds found their way into their new owners' minds. She watched as each Ballastian slowly closed their eyes. She watched as each fell into a heavy, heavy sleep.

"I love you," she said, so softly that Mayhap barely heard the words scraping past her lips.

Mayhap looked at Seekatrix as the images disappeared. "She gave us droomhunds because she *loved* us?"

Seekatrix whimpered, still tucked against her with his face hidden.

And then the door to the Office of Residents' Concerns began to rattle.

The pages of the contract fluttered like frightened bats. As they spread apart, Mayhap grabbed the last page—the one her parents had written on. Their note was torn, ruined, but this was also something from them, something they had touched. She folded it up and tucked it into her sleeve. She tied the ribbon around her wrist so that nothing would fall out. Then she stood, holding Seekatrix.

"Who's there?" she called out.

The door only jangled more. Seekatrix was trembling, his heart pounding beside her heart.

The door's juddering grew louder and more insistent.

"This is ridiculous," said Mayhap. "It's a *door*, for

sleep's sake." She pulled it open—fast—expecting to see the Mysteriessa.

But on the other side of the door was Pavonine, her face stricken and splotchy, Peffiandra shivering beside her.

CHAPTER

Thirteen

"I followed the crinkles in the carpet," whimpered Pavonine. "Except the door was locked, and I was so worried. I'm sorry for fighting with you, May—" She looked behind Mayhap into the Office of Residents' Concerns. "What—*is* this place?" she asked.

"Remember I told you about *The Book of Records*?" said Mayhap. "The book about the families who lived here before? Well, this is where they made their agreement with the house official, signed the papers. Once they'd signed, they found out what had been taken from them."

Pavonine stepped past Mayhap, Peffiandra at her heels.

"I'm sorry," said Pavonine again, bursting into tears. She covered her face with her hands. Peffiandra licked her ankle as if to comfort her. "I just don't know what to do."

Mayhap put her arms around her sister as Seekatrix curled his body around Peffiandra in a sort of droomhund hug. "Pav, is Winnow sleeping now?"

"She's not sleeping exactly. But she is lying still. She keeps saying your name. She's trying to tell me something, but she can't get it out."

Mayhap looked into Pavonine's tired eyes. She couldn't help but think of the contract's memory, of how they had all been so desperate to sleep. They had to look after themselves if they were going to figure this out. "Are you hungry, Pav?" she said.

"I *am* hungry."

"I thought you might be. Why don't we go to our bedroom and ask the house for a nice breakfast. Anything you like. And I'll tell you about all the things I've found out. And then afterward, we can have a nap with Winnow, all right? And maybe, when we wake up, we can find a solution together."

It seemed *wrong* to eat and sleep when Winnow was still so ill. But even people fighting to keep their sisters alive had to eat and sleep. Otherwise they wouldn't be able to help. Pavonine nodded in a determined, stubborn way that made Mayhap want to kiss her cheeks.

She decided then that she really would tell Pavonine everything—Mysteriessa and all. The Mysteriessa had lied to her. The Mysteriessa could not be trusted. Mayhap was not going to leave Pavonine out of anything from now on. From now on, they had to work together.

Winnow was lying in the sisters' crescent-shaped bed. Her eyes flicked open and closed, and her lips moved soundlessly. Her face and neck were completely silver. When Mayhap looked at her, a numb cold took over her body, and she couldn't feel her fingertips.

So she looked at Pavonine instead.

Pavonine sat on her chaise longue, and Mayhap followed suit. Their droomhunds lay at their feet.

The wallpaper in their bedroom had always shown figures against a backdrop of silver, but now Mayhap found herself peering at its details. The figures were girls, and the silver bent around them.

Every image in the house seemed like a symbol—or a threat.

Mayhap was shaken out of her thoughts by Pavonine's soft voice: "May? What are you going to have to eat?"

"Oh," said Mayhap. "You go ahead. I don't know what I feel like yet."

Pavonine requested a cup of hot chocolate and a cheese sandwich.

Mayhap squinted at her. "Hot chocolate and *cheese*? How is it possible that you can have those two things together?"

Pavonine only shrugged. She thought chocolate went with everything. It made Mayhap laugh—but only a little, because she was suddenly very aware of Winnow again, half asleep and just outside her vision, groaning faintly.

The food appeared on a little rose gold tray, which Pavonine placed on her lap. She looked cheerful for the first time in twelve hours. She lifted the sandwich with both hands and bit into it, then slurped her hot chocolate loudly. "May?" she asked.

"Yes, Pav?"

"Why is some magic good and other magic—*not* good?"

"What do you mean?"

"I mean, this sandwich"—she held the sandwich aloft—"is a kind of magic. The house gave it to me. It appeared out of nowhere."

"Right," said Mayhap.

"But the grass's magic is different."

Mayhap thought instantly of the Mysteriessa. Her magic was different, too.

"So why is the one good and the other bad?" asked Pavonine.

Mayhap ached for her parents to be sitting with them. She wanted *them* to answer the question.

But as she thought about Pavonine's question, she realized she had an answer. It wasn't something she knew with her mind; it was something she knew with the parts of her that were wordless. She knew it with her toes, with her fingertips.

"It's not that the magic is bad or good in itself," she said to Pavonine. "The magic itself is like any other tool—like a knife, or a hammer, or electricity. It's what the magic is *used for* that makes it good or bad. The house's magic is a helping magic. It looks after us. But the grass's magic"—*or the Mysteriessa's magic,* thought Mayhap—"is a taking magic. It is used to steal from us, and from others."

Winnow moaned, as though in agreement.

"That makes sense," said Pavonine, and Mayhap was satisfied with her answer for a moment.

But the more she pondered the Mysteriessa, the more that satisfaction evaporated. Because the Mysteriessa's magic was not only a taking magic. She did take from every resident of Straygarden Place, but she also gave them the house to live in, and she had given the Ballastians droomhunds when they couldn't sleep. Mayhap didn't know if she was good or bad. Maybe she was both.

Pavonine took a big sip of hot chocolate. "Are you going to ask the house for your food, May? Then you can tell me what you've found while we eat."

"Of course. I completely forgot," said Mayhap. Feeling lazy, she said, "I'll have my favorite breakfast. And a cup of Earl Grey tea."

The food appeared on a wooden tray, carved with birds' nests and inlaid with mother-of-pearl. It hovered in front of Mayhap before she placed it carefully on her lap.

But the house had made a mistake.

It had not given her a single *pain au chocolat*—her favorite breakfast. Instead, a bowl of steaming cinnamon porridge sat on the tray.

The house had never made an error like this before.

And even though it was only food—food that smelled perfectly fine—panic crept across Mayhap's scalp as though her hair were full of ants.

Pavonine hadn't noticed—she was too busy cooing

at Peffiandra. When she finally looked up, she said, "What?"

"The house gave me the wrong breakfast," said Mayhap. "I asked for my favorite, and it . . ." She gestured at her bowl.

"What is it? Porridge? You don't mind porridge. I rather like it, too. It smells nice."

"Pavonine, that's not the point." Mayhap shoved the tray off her lap, and it landed on the floor, and Seekatrix jumped with fright. The porridge seeped into the carpet.

"May!" said Pavonine. "Why don't you ask the house for your favorite again? I'm sure it was only . . ."

But Mayhap felt as though she were walking in the dark without a lamp. She looked past Pavonine's shoulder. She couldn't possibly make Pavonine understand how terrible this entirely insignificant thing had made her feel.

Winnow woke up, crying again, speaking in garbled and hurried fragments.

The house began to clean the mess Mayhap had made.

Mayhap watched as Seekatrix and Peffiandra played, wrestling and growling. She couldn't eat anything now. She could hardly think. "Let's go to sleep,

Pav," she said. "We'll feel better if we do. And then I can tell you everything." She stood and moved toward the bed, her head full of frantic fog.

"May?"

"Hmmm?" said Mayhap.

"We have to brush the droomhunds first."

Mayhap stopped beside the bed. "Oh, yes," she said, sniffing and wiping her nose with the back of her hand.

She looked at her feet to meet eyes with Seekatrix, but he and Peffiandra were still playing, and then they were speeding off, out of the bedroom, running abreast and barking, and there was nothing left to do but to fetch them back.

CHAPTER

Fourteen

Mayhap and Pavonine found the droomhunds in their father's old study, wrestling on the moss-green rug. The walls were covered in dark-blue silk, little silver stars stitched into it. The curtains were drawn, making the room feel like a cave. Lamps glowed dimly on the walls. Their father's desk was untouched, his collection of bat skeletons arranged on shadowed shelves behind it.

The tiny bones made Mayhap's skin tingle. She was still shaken from the porridge incident, and she didn't feel like being inside the dark shell of her father's once-favorite place. Her thoughts were loose in her head.

She grabbed at Seekatrix, who was wriggling about on the carpet with Peffiandra, but he scrambled away, his clipped nails skittering on the polished marble floor. Peffiandra darted off, too, hiding underneath the armchair behind the desk.

Pavonine sat on the floor, cross-legged, and called to her droomhund, and Peffiandra ran to her immediately. Mayhap wished Seekatrix would do the same, but something had come over him. He was running in zigzags so that she couldn't pick him up. Just as she thought she'd cornered him, he ran past her so quickly that her fingers only brushed his fluffy back, grasping at air.

Frustration burned in her throat. "Seeka," she moaned, standing straight with her hands on her hips. "Please. We don't have time for this."

She followed him behind the desk, where he sat panting. He barked twice and looked up.

"Seekatrix," said Mayhap, "stop!" She stamped her foot.

He wouldn't. He carried on growling, barking, growling some more. These were not warning sounds or sounds of fright. They were sounds that said, *I have had enough of you being upset. I want to play.*

"May," said Pavonine. "Tell him to stop."

Peffiandra was huddled in her arms.

"I'm trying," said Mayhap. She kneeled beside her droomhund. "What is it, Seeka?" she said.

He looked up and whined.

Mayhap followed his gaze to the bat skeletons. "I think he wants the bones," she said.

Pavonine only yawned.

Mayhap sighed. Perhaps if she gave him one of the skeletons, he would stop barking.

"All right, boy," she said, dragging the armchair over to the shelves.

She stood on it and peered into the uppermost shelf. The bat bones were connected by wire as thin as strands of spiders' silk. It made her shudder, touching them. Something churned within her. "Hmmm," she said. "Which shall I choose?"

Seekatrix wagged his tail.

She looked into the second-highest shelf.

The bones were the color of piano keys, as delicate as twigs. They made her think of her own bones, and Seekatrix's bones, too. *Do droomhunds have bones?* she wondered.

She put her hand over one of the little skeletons, saying a silent apology to her father.

And that's when she saw the secret drawer at the back of the shelf: a square that sat apart from the rest, a little handle. She tugged at it, releasing a held breath when it opened easily.

Seekatrix whined again. Mayhap held the bat skeleton in her hand, and the droomhund hopped up onto the chair and took it into his mouth gently. He lay down on the rug and began to chew it.

Mayhap reached into the secret drawer. Her fingers found something glossy. She took hold of it and pulled.

"What's that, May?" said Pavonine, who had come to stand beside the chair, holding Peffiandra under one arm.

"It's a—photograph," said Mayhap breathlessly, sitting down on the armchair.

Pavonine leaned over her. "A photograph? Of what?"

Mayhap held the photograph up for Pavonine to see. "It's—*me*," she said. "Me—with a droomhund."

The picture showed Mayhap's form, a brightness against a backdrop of shadows. The droomhund almost faded into the gray background.

"Is that Seekatrix?" said Pavonine, looking closer.

The photograph trembled in Mayhap's hand. "No, this dog is different. Its eyes—it's a different dog. A completely different dog."

"Oh," said Pavonine. The word sounded like a breath. "That must be your other droomhund, May."

"My *other* droomhund?"

102

Pavonine took the photograph out of Mayhap's hand. "Winnow told me. She remembers it. It was before Mamma and Pappa left—just before. When you were five, your droomhund died. And then you got a new one. Seeka. He just—arrived. They found him in your bed, curled up on the pillow. Winnow said she shouldn't have told me. Mamma and Pappa told her not to tell us, because we would only be upset and worried. She asked me never to tell you." Pavonine looked at Mayhap guiltily.

Mayhap snatched the photograph back and stared at it, as though doing so would explain everything. But the more she stared at it, the less she felt she knew.

"I don't understand," she said. "How did my droomhund—*this* droomhund—die?" Seekatrix and Peffiandra had fallen conspicuously silent.

Pavonine squinted. "Winnow said the grass took it. A window was open, and . . ."

Mayhap's head was a pan of rising dough. Here was the smell-of-coffee feeling again. The feeling she'd had when Tutto gave her the catalog card with *The Collected Diaries of Quiverity Edevane* printed on it. She was being buried. She was swallowing too much soil. She couldn't breathe.

Silver grass coming for her—

She remembered its tightness around her wrists, its softness against her cheeks.

Pavonine was looking at her with frightened eyes. "Mayhap? Winnow said it was only an accident—"

"No," said Mayhap. "I don't think any of this is an accident." She stuffed the photograph up her sleeve. "Pav, go check on Winnow, please. Brush Peffiandra and get some rest. I need to do something."

CHAPTER

Fifteen

"Mysteriessa?" said Mayhap, stepping into the conservatory with Seekatrix.

Daylight shone through the grass outside, making the glass walls look like mother-of-pearl, and bats hung from branches overhead like ornaments on dainty chains. Mayhap thought of the bones in her father's study. A tickle crept up her spine.

She untied the ribbon around her wrist and carefully removed the photograph, the last page of the contract, and the scraps of her parents' note. She held them against her chest like playing cards, moving through the conservatory until she came face-to-face with the white-eyed girl.

"You found me," said the Mysteriessa. In the pale light, her eyes looked waxy, as though they'd been carved from marble.

"What happened to my first droomhund?" Mayhap said, holding out the photograph.

The Mysteriessa squinted. "Where did you get that?" she said.

"Never mind where I found it," said Mayhap. "Tell me what happened. Tell me the truth."

The girl took the photograph from her and stared at it. "Lovely thing, he was," she said wistfully.

"My sister says the grass took him," said Mayhap. "Winnow told her. Why don't I remember that?"

The Mysteriessa smoothed the front of her dress. She was still wearing the same glistening garment, and the silver thread caught the sun's light. It hurt to look at it. Her hair was so white that it appeared translucent. "You need to sleep, Mayhap. You're panicking because you're tired. Sleep is so important for the mind."

"Is that why you gave our family droomhunds? After you took our sleep away?" said Mayhap. She spoke as though she wore armor, not a flimsy dressing gown and slippers.

The Mysteriessa's face turned pink as cooked ham.

"I went to the Office of Residents' Concerns," said Mayhap. "You said it was the grass who took things from the families. But it was you. Pavonine said the

106

grass took my first droomhund. But that's not true, either, is it? Tell me what happened."

The Mysteriessa of Straygarden Place pursed her dry lips.

The silence was like oxygen, feeding the fire within Mayhap. "The contract showed me," she said. "You let my parents in here—you let all of us in here—and you made them sign away their sleep." She tried to unfold the last page of the contract, to hold it up for the Mysteriessa to see. As she did, the pieces of her parents' shredded note fluttered to the floor.

She crouched to pick them up, smoothing the contract before arranging the fragments of the note to make sure she hadn't lost one. It was then that she noticed the handwriting. On the contract, Cygnet's script was rectangular and resolute, Bellwether's swooping and melodramatic. In the note, however, the letters were curled tightly, and slanted to the left.

Mayhap looked up at the Mysteriessa. "The grass has nothing to do with anything, does it? *You* took my parents, didn't you? *You* took my first droomhund. And now you're going to take Winnow."

"That's not true," said the Mysteriessa. "Your parents *chose* to leave you."

"According to the note they left, yes," said Mayhap,

standing up and leaving the pieces of paper on the floor like scattered autumn leaves. "But they didn't write it, did they?"

"They—"

"The handwriting in the note doesn't match either script in the contract." Mayhap spat the words out. "So either they didn't write on the contract or they didn't write the note. And since I saw them in the contract's vision—I *saw* them sign it—I'm more inclined to believe the latter."

The Mysteriessa only stared at Mayhap, her eyes like two distant moons.

"*You* wrote it, didn't you? They never wanted to leave. You *made* them leave."

"Mayhap, I—"

"What happened?" said Mayhap, snatching the photograph out of the Mysteriessa's hand and shoving it in her face. She whispered through gritted teeth, "What—did—you—*do*?"

The Mysteriessa stood up straighter and clasped her hands. "Mayhap Ballastian," she said, "you would do well to respect me."

The words shook Mayhap's heart like a rattle. "*Respect* you?" A laugh like a cough left her mouth.

"Seekatrix," called the Mysteriessa.

The droomhund walked over to her, his tail wagging.

"Leave him alone!" cried Mayhap.

"Seeka," the Mysteriessa sang. She picked him up and held him in her arms, stroking his head. "You know I called the droomhunds, don't you? I called them out of the night, and they came to me."

Mayhap lowered the photograph in her hand.

"Did it occur to you that I can make them do anything I like?" said the Mysteriessa.

"Please," Mayhap said. "I'm sorry for getting angry. Please leave him alone."

"You need to get some rest, Mayhap," said the Mysteriessa. "Trust me. I know you. I've known you your whole life." She took a step toward Mayhap, Seekatrix balanced in her arms.

Sweet Seeka, who was trying to lick the Mysteriessa's cheek. Sweet, sweet Seeka.

"No," said Mayhap. "Whatever you're going to do, don't—"

The Mysteriessa put her mouth close to Seekatrix's ear. "Time to sleep darkly, Seeka. *Now.*"

She threw him into the air, toward Mayhap, and he leaped at her, leaped into her mind, burrowing into her head frantically, and she couldn't think, couldn't stand. Her head filled with a fuzzy darkness, and she was falling.

The marble floor rose beneath her. The sleepy chirps of bats swept over her.

And then everything went black, as though someone had drawn a curtain over the world.

CHAPTER

Sixteen

Seekatrix's unbrushed fur prickled the edges of Mayhap's mind. Color, image, sound, and smell—all of them hurried through her like trains through tunnels.

In her dreams, she held white bats in her hands, their pink and open mouths like the fragile insides of flowers.

In her dreams, she dug deep holes in a quiet garden and placed the bats into them. She covered them with soil as moist as pudding.

The bats' clawed feet needled the earth. They threw the dirt off their backs, spread their fleshy wings, multiplied.

No matter how many of them she buried, they always came back up, screeching, until the whole sky was full of them.

She closed her hands, and when she opened them again, her palms were silver.

CHAPTER

Seventeen

Mayhap woke in the conservatory, Seekatrix tumbling out of her mind like a stream of black smoke. The bats were swooping back and forth above her. She sat up and rubbed her temples.

"I'm sorry, Seeka," she said, holding him tightly. "I don't know how she did that. But we're all right. We're all right now."

The silver grass was tinted with a distinctly crepuscular mauve. It was evening. She had been asleep for an entire day. While Winnow was sick and in danger. She had to go to her sisters. She had to do something.

She stood up on trembling legs. Her ears slowly adjusted to the world of waking.

And then screams echoed through the house like thrums of discordant music.

Mayhap moved toward the conservatory's door, her vision smeared like a misty window, and Seekatrix followed her.

She found Winnow and Pavonine near their bedroom, around a few bends of carpet.

"May!" called Pavonine. "She was fine, I promise. Sleeping and everything. And then something happened, and she got upset again. I couldn't stop her—"

Winnow was slumped against the wall. There were fallen mirrors all around her, shards of glass glittering like sequins. She was covering her eyes. She was sobbing. She bent forward as though she were in agony. Her hands were cut. Her blood was as red as the lipstick their mother used to wear.

"W-Winnow?" said Pavonine. She stepped toward her, holding a hand up to show Mayhap that she should stay back.

Mayhap didn't need to be told not to go near Winnow. But it still stung that Winnow could not be near her without becoming frightened and violent.

Pavonine approached Winnow and crouched beside her, stroking her cheek, and Winnow grew calmer.

It'll be fine, thought Mayhap. *Pavonine will calm her down, and I'll—I'll—*

Mayhap had no idea what to do next. Maybe she would talk to Tutto again. Maybe she would find the Mysteriessa and apologize, try to get more details out of her—

But Winnow did not calm down, not like last time.

She bared her teeth at Pavonine and pushed her away—a flat hand against each of Pavonine's shoulders. Pavonine fell back, winded. Red dribbled from her finger. She'd cut it on the glass-littered floor. Peffiandra ran to her and licked her face.

Winnow's wet eyes leaked silver-tinted tears as she stepped—slowly, deliberately—toward Mayhap, holding out one hand as if she wanted her sister to take it.

Mayhap held her breath as the distance between them shrank.

"May—" whimpered Pavonine.

"Shhh, Pav," said Mayhap. Winnow took her hand. And for a brief lemon-drop moment, Mayhap had come home again. Her sister loved her again. "Winn," she said. "Winnow. Let me help you."

Winnow's bottom lip wobbled. Up close, Mayhap

could see that she was entirely silver, from the tips of her eyelashes and ears right down to her bare toes and the slips of her fingers.

"Winnow," said Mayhap. "It's all right. You're going to be all right."

Little liar.

Winnow pulled Mayhap toward her, hugging her, and Mayhap wrapped her arms around her sister. Her hair smelled of wanderroot blossoms. Everything Mayhap had been feeling up until this point—fear, rage, confusion—flooded out of her in the form of tears. The tears soaked into her sister's hair.

Distantly, Mayhap could hear Pavonine. "May— she's got—"

But it was too late.

Winnow caught hold of Mayhap's forearm—her fingers pinching so tightly that Mayhap couldn't pull away. In her other hand, Winnow held a shard of mirror. In a moment she had made a clean cut through Mayhap's skin.

Mayhap hissed and brought her arm to her lips. She tasted earth. And, when she lowered her arm again, her blood wasn't red—not like Pavonine's, and not like Winnow's. No—hers was *silver.*

I told you not to meddle, came a voice—the voice of the Mysteriessa. Mayhap looked around, but she couldn't see her.

She clamped her hand over the wound, but it was no use—the blood, the silver, was seeping between her fingers.

"Pav," said Mayhap, her voice shaky.

"May?" said Pavonine. "May, why is your blood— silver?" Each word was a splinter. Fear made her cheeks white.

"I don't know," said Mayhap. But she *did* know, deep in the root of her being, that she wasn't sick.

This was something else. There was something wrong.

"But—silver is bad. Silver is the grass. Are you sick, too? May? Answer me."

Mayhap looked at the palms of her hands. "I don't know," she said again. But she knew that Winnow, sick as she was, still had blood that was raspberry red.

"Let me see," said Pavonine.

Mayhap pushed her sister away. "I have to—I have to go—I'm sorry—"

Winnow stared at her with flat, unyielding eyes. With smug victory.

"Where do you have to go?" asked Pavonine. She

began to cry. "You can't get sick, too, May. Please—let me see—"

"You can't help me!" Mayhap screamed.

She hadn't wanted to treat Pavonine badly. But the shame in her, prickly as winter trees, made her want to bite. It made her want to hide.

She had to get away from her sisters.

She had to get away from their eyes.

CHAPTER

Eighteen

Mayhap stumbled along in the dark, clutching her wounded arm. Somehow, she had lost her slippers, and the carpets were soft beneath her feet. She could have asked the house to light its lamps, but she didn't. She did not want to catch a glimpse of her face in any mirror.

She walked and walked, and the hallways seemed to sway and twist. Seekatrix skipped at her side, nipping at her dressing gown, but Mayhap ignored him and kept moving. She didn't know where she was going. She only knew that if she stood still, she would have to think about the silver patch of blood on her arm.

She asked the house if it could help her with the cut. More than anything, she wanted to stop the bleeding. She blinked, and when she opened her eyes, she could feel a bandage wrapped tightly around her arm.

The thought of the silver staining the sleeve of her dressing gown made her nauseous, and she took it off, leaving it on the floor. And even though she wore only a thin nightgown underneath, she was warm—from the blood pulsing through her, from her pounding heart. Her *silver* heart.

She pressed the thought to the back of her mind and she walked. But that word kept coming back to her: *silver, silver, silver.*

The passages seemed to widen and shrink. She walked until she stepped on something—something small and sharp, digging into the arch of her foot.

"Ouch," she said in the dark.

But she didn't want to look. If she looked, there might be more silver.

She kept walking until she stepped on *another* object, this one smoother. She halted, and Seekatrix copied her. His body brushed her leg.

"Please," she said to the house, still whispering, "some light. A little."

The house lit the lamps along the walls dimly, and their strange, colorful shapes came into view—and so did the thing at her feet.

It was a small compact mirror, all gold on the out-side. Mayhap opened it and felt something shift within her, like wind blowing through an open window. She snapped it closed.

Then she saw that there were more objects, set in a line all down the hallway, like joints in a long, long finger.

She stumbled back onto a tiny jewelry box studded with sapphires.

"What is this?" she whispered.

Seekatrix was glued against her leg, wagging his tail nervously.

Mayhap began to walk slowly again, picking up the little trinkets as she went. Pocket watches, snuffboxes, little jars emptied of jam.

She picked up a half-empty perfume bottle and lifted it to her nose. And found that the bottle did not contain only eau de toilette. The bottle contained— what was it?

It was . . .

It was . . .

Mayhap was sure that it was *quiet*.

The sort of quiet that settled into you when you were tucked somewhere warm, listening to the pattering of rain. Peace. Peace from the inside out—that's what the bottle held. Mayhap placed it back where she had found it.

Then it occurred to her: these must be the things the Mysteriessa had stolen from families. Odd things, like memory, and music, and solitude.

She followed the pathway of treasures until she came to a twisting staircase.

It was narrow. It had boxes and jars and little tins on each of its high, steep steps.

"They mean for me to follow them," said Mayhap, dazed and exhausted.

Seekatrix seemed nervous, but he scuttled up the stairs.

Mayhap followed him to the third floor of the house.

The floor the girls never went up to.

The old servants' quarters.

Seekatrix stopped at one of the doors. Mayhap opened it.

Tutto had told Pavonine about the servants—about how Straygarden Place had once had a staff of sixty. Pavonine had shown Mayhap the stairs that led up to the third floor. Winnow, Mayhap, and Pavonine had stood at the foot of those stairs, staring at the wrought iron balustrade that curled its way up alongside them. But Mayhap had never wanted to put her hand on the balustrade, had never wanted to hear her shoes clicking on the rising marble.

The third floor was not for her.

Her bones had known it.

Only now—now that the strewn stolen things had *made* her come—she knew, somehow, that it *was* meant for her, that there was something tying her to this place, to this room with its slim, tidy bed and its heart-shaped windows, silvered with nighttime grass.

On the dresser was another, single box. It looked like a ring box.

Mayhap opened it.

It looked empty, but it wasn't.

It was filled with belonging.

The sensation hit her like a familiar smell. It was like knowing someone had come home—an opened door, fresh air rushing in behind them.

Inside the box was the feeling of speaking and having someone listen—really *listen*. It was the feeling of someone looking into your eyes and knowing you—every part of you.

Mayhap could have called it belonging, or she could have called it love, or she could have called it family. Whatever it was, it hit her in her stomach, the feeling of it, and she fell to her knees. Tears ran down her cheeks. She retched and sobbed.

She lay on the floor shaking while Seekatrix licked her face.

She remembered how Peffiandra had found a box and chewed the lid off. Pavonine hadn't been able to stop laughing. Now Mayhap understood that Peffiandra had found a box full of *laughter*—laughter that the Mysteriessa had stolen from some unsuspecting family.

I need to close that ring box, she thought. But she couldn't move her hands.

And then the shape of a person clouded her sight, and she knew the Mysteriessa had come.

CHAPTER

Nineteen

It was the Mysteriessa who closed the ring box—
clapping it shut like the tiniest of doors. "That's not
for you," she said, as though Mayhap were a toddler
reaching for a chocolate éclair. "You should know that's
not for you."

Mayhap wriggled her fingers. She found that she
could open her eyes. She found that she could sit up.
Seekatrix crawled into her arms. "You're a liar," said
Mayhap. The cut on her forearm was stinging. She stood,
holding her droomhund, even though her body shook.

The Mysteriessa seemed unmoved by the insult.
"You see all these things I've taken? I can take
more. I can take anything I want from you. If you don't
stop meddling, Mayhap, that's what I'm going to do."

"I can't just pretend that nothing's happened. Not
when you're making Winnow sick."

"I did not make her sick!" screeched the Mysteriessa. The next words were softer: "I made her silent."

"Silent?" said Mayhap. "Why?"

"You don't understand what it is to lose everything," the Mysteriessa said.

"So tell me," said Mayhap.

The Mysteriessa scoffed. "Do you know why these rooms are empty?" she said. "Because they all *left*. The servants my father hired. Each and every one of them left me, left a girl alone here—can you believe that?"

Mayhap looked at the tidy bed. The windows. The dresser.

"The cook who made our porridge in the mornings, and our nanny—"

"The house didn't care for you?" asked Mayhap.

"The house only looks after the families who live here because of me," snapped the Mysteriessa. When Mayhap looked at her blankly, she continued. "My name was Quiverity Edevane before I became the Mysteriessa of Straygarden Place."

The Collected Diaries of Quiverity Edevane. "Your diaries—"

"Never mind that!" said the Mysteriessa. "I'm trying to tell you a story, Mayhap Ballastian. The grass took my family from me. It snaked around them and pulled them out of the house. They screamed and screamed, but it didn't listen. It pulled them underground. And the servants all thought it was my fault." She gestured around the room. "As if a twelve-year-old girl could kill her entire family. They left me, one by one, and I was alone in this big house, with nothing but magic to keep me company. I had so much magic, Mayhap. For the first time in my life. And I didn't know what to do with it."

"So you made the house look after you," said Mayhap.

Tears ran down the Mysteriessa's cheeks. "Stop. Meddling!" she shrieked through gritted teeth. "And I will let Winnow be. Stop looking for answers, and she won't get worse."

But Mayhap knew she couldn't do that.

"She's my sister," she said, pleading. "I don't want her not to get *worse*—I want her to get *better.* I can't stop—"

"You will!" said the Mysteriessa. "Or you will lose everything, as I did. *We* will lose everything."

"I don't understand—"

"Of course you don't! You don't know the cost of it. The cost of light is darkness, Mayhap. And do you know what the cost of having a family is? Hiding who you really are."

126

Mayhap had never, ever, had to hide who she was. She had lost her parents too young to have to hide anything from them, and her sisters had always known her every secret. "It doesn't have to be that way," she said. "Please. Let Winnow be, and—"

The Mysteriessa laughed bitterly. "You haven't seen," she said, "that everything I'm doing is to protect you. To protect *us*."

"*Us?*" Mayhap was tired of how the Mysteriessa tiptoed around secrets. Mayhap wanted to *know*. She wanted to know now. Before the silver took over Winnow. Before it was too late.

If she could only push the Mysteriessa a little bit more—

"You're a coward," Mayhap said.

"I'm not scared, I'm—"

"You are scared!"

"I am not!" said the Mysteriessa, covering her ears. "I'm trying to protect you!"

"I don't want you to protect me," said Mayhap. "I want you to make Winnow better."

"I can't . . ." whimpered the Mysteriessa. "I can't . . ." She backed away and fell onto the narrow bed, curling up like a puppy. She began to sing quietly.

The song was so familiar. It was as though it wasn't

coming from the Mysteriessa but off Mayhap's own tongue.

Then she made out the words: *Think of an animal, think of a place. Think of a person, think of a face.* The guessing game she had always played with her sisters. Coming out of the Mysteriessa's mouth.

The words filled her with dread, but she was desperate to know the truth. She was desperate to make Winnow better. She had to keep trying, no matter what. She would try another tactic. She would try gentleness. She would get the Mysteriessa to talk.

"Quiverity," Mayhap whispered, letting Seekatrix hop to the floor. "Tell me your favorite food, and I will ask the house for it. That'll make you feel better, won't it?" She touched the back of the Mysteriessa's head, her silver-streaked hair.

A long silence.

Then the Mysteriessa sniffed. "Cinnamon porridge," she said. "My favorite food is cinnamon porridge."

Mayhap stepped back. "The house gave me *your* favorite breakfast," she said.

Seekatrix began to bark.

The Mysteriessa sat up. "You're putting it together,
aren't you?" she said, her tone as buttery as brioche. She
giggled. "Think of an animal, think of a place. Think of
a person, think of a face."

Mayhap backed away more, knocking over a vase.
It cracked, and sunlight streamed into the room.

The Mysteriessa had stolen *sunlight* from someone.

"I still don't understand," said Mayhap. "Why
would the house give me your favorite breakfast?"

"Because," said the Mysteriessa, "you are me."

Mayhap wanted to laugh—the words were so
absurd—but she found that she couldn't. "What do

you mean? You're Quiverity Edevane. You're the Mysteriessa—"

"I mean," said the Mysteriessa, "that you are not a Ballastian sister. You never were. I *made* you, Mayhap. I made you out of dirt and bats' lungs. Out of the darkness of the sky and the silk of the moon. A sprinkling of coffee grounds for your freckles." The Mysteriessa held up her two white hands. "I made you with my magic, and I dug a hole deep in your heart—a hole I could nestle into. So that I could live within you. Live *through* you. It's been so long since I had a sister, Mayhap. You must understand."

Mayhap couldn't breathe. Her blood was silver—silver like the grass. Silver like the streaks in the Mysteriessa's hair.

"I used to love the grass," said the Mysteriessa. "I used to love it more than anything, and it loved me back. I would spend hours running through it. It would rush against my skin. One day it asked me if I wanted to be a queen. A queen, like the ones in the stories it told me. And I said yes. I had settled down into the grass for a nap, and it told me it would need to take something from me—to make space for the magic to go in." Tears streamed down her cheeks. "I said yes, and I drifted off—that beautiful, hushing color all around me, the grass giving shape to the wind. I woke to my family's cries. I woke to see the grass pulling them beneath the ground. My mother. My father. My two sisters. And then they were gone. It only took a few moments, but those moments—they were everything. Do you know what I mean, Mayhap?"

Mayhap knew exactly what the Mysteriessa meant.

"The servants left," continued the Mysteriessa. "I was alone. I had only magic to keep me company. I asked the house to look after me. But I became lonely, so lonely. I invited families here and stole from them— silence, good tastes, warmth. I stole from the families who lived here so that the magic could touch them. So that the house could look after them. I stole because I had been stolen from. Because stealing felt good. I stole to watch them suffer, as I had suffered. And then the Ballastians came along, and I couldn't stand to watch them suffer. They were so much like my mother and my father, so much like my sisters."

The room grew smaller and smaller.

If Mayhap searched—if she really *looked*—she could find the hole the Mysteriessa had made. It was in her heart, a little to the left. She could find it the way a tongue finds a cavity in a tooth. It was there. And if it was there, the Mysteriessa was telling the truth. Mayhap *wasn't* a Ballastian. She wasn't even a Mayhap. She was *nothing*.

Worse.

She was a monster. A beast made of dirt and bats' lungs and scratches of sky.

"I know what happened," said Mayhap.

The Mysteriessa crossed her arms as though she appreciated the challenge.

"There were three of us," said Mayhap.

"Hmmm?" said the Mysteriessa.

"There were three of us. You had two sisters, too, just like us."

"Just like *them*," said the Mysteriessa.

"You didn't want us to leave. Eventually we'd have left, if we couldn't sleep. You wanted us to stay. That's why you gave us the droomhunds. The contract showed me how you called the droomhunds and brought them to us. You said you loved us. Because we reminded you of your lost family. Three girls. A mother. A father."

"So?" said the Mysteriessa.

"It wasn't enough," said Mayhap. "It wasn't enough for you to live beside us, hiding in the house unseen.

You wanted to be one of us—one of them." The word *them* stuck in Mayhap's throat like a fish's bone. "So you made—*me*."

It all fell into place now. The empty feeling that sometimes surfaced in her heart. Her hatred of the smell of coffee. The taste of earth.

Her nightmare of being buried wasn't a fear; it was a memory.

"You made me," said Mayhap, "and you buried me. You made me in the soil, among the silver. You brought me to life. I coughed out the black earth. I coughed it out at your feet. You slipped into my heart. And I became the new Mayhap, a new Ballastian girl—" Mayhap's mind was filled with foggy desperation. "Winnow found out. That's why you made her sick. Because she was going to say something—tell Pavonine. She was going to break it all apart. You hurt Winnow to protect me. To protect us. It was because of me, it was me all along, making Winnow sick, hurting her . . ."

The room spun.

"Yes," said the Mysteriessa. "Yes, clever creature. And you think your sisters love you entirely. How could they possibly? When you don't even know who you are."

Mayhap found herself on her knees. She was

coughing. She was coughing up silver blood. "What did you do to the other Mayhap? The middle Ballastian sister? What did you do to my parents?" she said.

Seekatrix tried to lick her cheek, but she pushed him away.

"Enough," said the Mysteriessa.

She clicked her fingers, and Mayhap felt heat bloom through her. She felt as though she had been thrown down a long, twisting set of stairs. When she opened her eyes, though, she was in her bedroom. She was still on her knees, and Seekatrix was shaking beside her.

Pavonine was standing by the bed, and Winnow was writhing, her skin as silver as a moonlit lake. The little ormolu clock on the mantel ticked and ticked.

"What happened—" Mayhap began to say.

But the Mysteriessa interrupted her.

"I let them hear your story, Mayhap," she said. "Now Pavonine knows who you really are. Just like Winnow does."

CHAPTER

Twenty-One

"Pavonine," said Mayhap. "I didn't know. I promise you."

Pavonine shook her head slowly, looking from Quiverity Edevane to Mayhap. "Stay away from me," she said, picking Peffiandra up and putting a hand on Winnow's silver shoulder.

Mayhap listened. She didn't want to frighten Pavonine any more than she already had. Seekatrix sat at her side, mirroring her. After a moment, Mayhap took one step forward, and Seekatrix did, too.

"Get back!" said Pavonine.

Mayhap froze. But she carried on talking. "Pav," she said. "I didn't know. You have to believe me. I didn't know any of this—"

"Don't lie to me!" Pavonine said, her mouth a twist of shock. "You kept sending me away. You kept telling me to look after Winnow. I thought it was because you wanted to figure things out on your own. But you never did figure anything out, did you, because you never had anything *to* figure out. You said you'd tell me everything, and then you made a scene about a bowl of porridge."

Mayhap peered into her own heart as if she were looking through a telescope. *Had* she known? Had she known why Winnow was sick? Had she known what she *was*?

No.

She couldn't have.

She hadn't.

She had been as confused as Pavonine. As scared as Winnow.

She hadn't done this on purpose.

But she was still the Mysteriessa's vessel. Her body was a traitor.

"Stay away from me, May—I can't even say your name. It isn't yours. You *stole* it."

"You're scaring your sister, Mayhap," said the Mysteriessa. There was a hint of joy in her words.

Mayhap put her hands up. "Pav, I'm going to—I'm going to go out into the hallway. You can come out when—when you're ready to talk."

Pavonine's face was hard.

Mayhap left the room with Seekatrix, and the Mysteriessa followed. When Mayhap looked around, the pale girl with silver hair was gone.

There was an iciness in Mayhap's lungs. The Mysteriessa had nestled into her chest again.

Mayhap wanted to rip her own heart out to be rid of her. She wanted to scream. Instead, she sank to the floor silently, her back against the wall. Seekatrix lay beside her.

Her head was a pack of wolves, and all her thoughts had sharp teeth.

Winnow knew.

Winnow had grown tired of obeying the rules. The rules they'd thought had come from their parents but had actually come from the Mysteriessa. Winnow had gone looking for answers. Somehow, Winnow had found out the truth.

Think of an animal, think of a place. Think of a person, think of a face.

The Mysteriessa had put that rhyme on Mayhap's tongue as a taunt. She was part animal, part place. Part person. She was the Mysteriessa's face.

Mayhap could not go back to guessing games and apple cake. There was no way to travel the ground that took a girl like her—a girl made of darkness and bats' lungs—back there, back to sister-whispers and lace-ruffled afternoons.

But she could try to make things better.

She could try to make *Winnow* better.

The Mysteriessa was not Mayhap. They were separate, like the yolk and the white of an egg. But living within someone's heart for nearly a decade had to leave some traces behind.

What trail have you scattered, Quiverity Edevane?

Mayhap closed her eyes. She sat up straight.

What happened? she asked herself. *What happened the night Winnow fell ill?*

A vision blinked into Mayhap's mind, flickering on and off.

She sat excruciatingly still, as though the memory were a frail baby-winged bat that would fly away if she frightened it.

Pavonine and Mayhap had gone to sleep, their droomhunds snuggled soundly in their minds, but Winnow paced the room, trying to decide what to do about the truth.

That's when the Mysteriessa unfurled from Mayhap's chest like steam from a kettle.

She formed herself at the foot of their bed, ragged in her silver dress. Winnow saw her, eyes wide. The Mysteriessa reached out a hand—

Winnow ran, bare feet on the carpet. She pushed their bedroom door open, escaping into the hallway. She asked the house to light the lamps.

The Mysteriessa made the lamps spark and go out.

Winnow shuddered, a breath in the dark.

"You know my secret," the Mysteriessa said in her high, sweet voice.

And Winnow, brave Winnow, said, "I know you took my sister away—and I know my parents left to find her. I know who you are."

The Mysteriessa grabbed at Winnow, but she ran away again.

In Mayhap's memory, the two of them looked like a pair of ghosts, two white dresses and four lungs breathing.

"You'll keep my secret," said the Mysteriessa. She sounded desperate, hungry.

"No, I won't," Winnow said.

The Mysteriessa pushed Winnow into another room—the one Mayhap and Pavonine had found her in. She wrestled her onto the bed.

Winnow fought, but the Mysteriessa was strong with magic.

Then the white-eyed girl took Evenflee into her arms and stroked him lovingly, speaking his name as though it were a spoon of elderflower syrup on her tongue.

Winnow held out a hand. "Don't hurt him, please—"

"I'm not going to hurt him," said the Mysteriessa. The next two words were growled: "Lie back."

"Please," said Winnow. Tears dribbled out the sides of her eyes as she jerked her head onto the pillow. "Don't hurt him—or Pavonine. Please."

"I would never hurt my sisters," said the Mysteriessa. "I love my sisters. I love them so much."

And with those words, she shoved Evenflee into Winnow's mind.

While Evenflee squirmed and fought and scratched inside Winnow's head, the Mysteriessa placed a hand over each one of Winnow's ears. When she pulled them away, Winnow's ears were leaking silver.

Sitting in the hallway a day later, Mayhap opened her eyes.

"Pav was right, Seeka. It's Evenflee," she said. "But he's not gone. He's caught in her mind. He's stuck. He's panicked. He's trying to get out. That's why she's in so much pain."

Seekatrix whined.

And, like clockwork, Pavonine opened the door.

Pavonine stood in the doorway, holding Winnow's hand. The house had dressed them in warm coats and leather boots. Pavonine wore every shade of gray. Winnow was in emerald.

Mayhap and Seekatrix got to their feet. "Pav," said Mayhap, breathless. "I know you're angry with me, but I have to tell you something."

Pavonine stood protectively in front of Winnow, who was barely awake on her feet and all silver. "*Angry* with you?" she said. "I'm not *angry* with you, Mayhap. I feel nothing for you. Nothing. You're a liar. You're a *lie*." Fear sparked beneath her anger. Mayhap could practically *see* it. She stepped aside as Pavonine took Winnow's hand and dragged her down the hallway.

"Where are you going?" she called. "Pavonine— please. You were right. About Evenflee. He's making her sick. He's trapped in her mind—"

Pavonine turned around, holding Winnow's hand tightly. "*You* are the one who made Winnow sick! Do you really think I'm going to listen to another word you say about how to make her better? Evenflee is gone. You probably got rid of him, just like you got rid of the real Mayhap and her droomhund." Mayhap stepped toward Pavonine, but Pavonine shouted, "Stay back!" and began to run. Winnow ran with her. Peffiandra followed.

I told you, said a voice. The Mysteriessa's voice. *The truth is a terrible, terrible thing. You'll never be loved by your sisters again. But at least, dear creature, you have me.*

Mayhap clawed at her chest, angry tears spilling onto her flushed cheeks. The Mysteriessa slinked like cool satin inside her heart.

You know where your sisters are going, don't you? In their pretty coats?

No.

They couldn't be.

But Mayhap had seen the fear in Pavonine's eyes, and she knew it was true.

CHAPTER

Twenty-Three

By the time Mayhap and Seekatrix arrived at the entrance hall, it was too late.

The enormous door was open, banging on its hinges. The silver grass hissed its tendrils against the wallpaper and the vaulted ceiling.

And Winnow and Pavonine were gone.

CHAPTER

Twenty-Four

Mayhap stood before the open front door.

The wind howled, and the grass howled, and she howled, too.

"Pavonine! Winnow!"

No good could come from stepping out into the grass—unless that good was saving your sisters. Unless that good was showing them you loved them more than anything, even if you were made of bats' lungs and soil and ground-up coffee beans.

Mayhap stood on the threshold between inside and out—between what she had always known and what lay waiting for her. The silver gathered around her. Her heart throbbed.

Something squeaked and shuffled behind her, and she turned around, thinking Seekatrix was up to something. But it was Tutto, circling on his wheels. Mayhap had never seen him outside the library before.

"Tutto?" she said. "What are you doing here?"

"Mayhap—don't go out there. You'll get hurt—your parents said not to go outside—" Tutto rammed back and forth.

"I have to, Tutto," she said.

"But you're not supposed to go outside," he said again. "It's one of the rules."

"Pavonine's out there, Tutto. And Winnow. I have to make sure they're—"

"You are not supposed to go outside!" he screeched.

"Tutto?" said Mayhap. "Are you all right?"

Tutto began to spin again, even quicker, his drawers rattling. His eyes split down the middle like dropped opals. He hummed and quivered.

"Tutto!" said Mayhap. "Tutto?"

She watched in horror as his body came apart in unraveling slices of silver, his drawers sliding out of his torso, the catalog cards flittering around him, until he was only coiled ribbons of metal, and little springs, and four wooden wheels dropped on the floor.

You should have listened to him, someone said within her.

The Mysteriessa.

Mayhap went numb.

She remembered Winnow's story about Tutto coming to life.

And she knew: the *Mysteriessa* had given Tutto life.

She had done it so that the hippopotamus could read Pavonine stories, could show the girls small kindnesses. Could nuzzle their hair and tell them everything would be fine.

The Mysteriessa had made him, and now she had destroyed him.

Mayhap screamed, running and kicking at Tutto's scattered parts.

She scooped Seekatrix under one arm and wrestled the grass away from the door, making an opening.

She leaped into the silver.

CHAPTER
Twenty-Five

The grass twisted its silvery twines around Mayhap's waist. Next: her ankles, her wrists. It tugged Seekatrix out of her arms.

To her surprise, though, she found it did not seem to want to hurt her or her droomhund. She had thought about screaming, but before she'd been able to, the grass had taken her up so carefully that she'd had nothing to scream about.

So she let the sea of it take her, carrying her into the sky, high and higher, until the roots of the wanderroot trees brushed her forehead like a blessing.

Mayhap kept her eyes open—open for Pavonine's gray coat, for Winnow's green one. She hoped the grass was handling them kindly, too. For a few long seconds, Mayhap could not see anything but rolling silver. But then she glimpsed a snatch of dark hair, a spot of emerald beside it.

"Pavonine," she said, under her breath. "Winnow."

The grass seemed to swallow them then, and Mayhap's stomach sank, because she had thought the grass had been peaceful—she had been so sure. But actually, now that she thought about it, it seemed—*hungry*.

It shimmered around her, smiling in its sly, silvery way. Mayhap knew that it was smiling. And it wasn't a friendly smile, either. It was the sort of smile you had on your face before you bit into something delicious.

"Pavonine," Mayhap tried to say, but her mouth was filled with grass, and she choked on it, spluttering.

"Ours, ours, ours," it hissed.

And it took her into its mouth.

CHAPTER

Twenty-Six

The grass had swallowed Mayhap.

And now the grass spat her out.

She landed on her back. On a surface as hard as marble. She felt her droomhund licking her face.

Pavonine spoke beside her. "Where are we?"

Mayhap wanted to see if Pavonine was all right. She wanted to talk to her.

She sat up, forced her eyes open.

And saw steps leading up to a large door. A grand house leaned over them, like a person inspecting an insect. Its hundreds of windows glimmered with moonlight. Pavonine was sitting, rubbing her elbow. Winnow was lying next to her, whimpering, still so silver.

The grass had brought them back to Straygarden Place—all three of them.

It had given them a chance to begin again.

Mayhap was about to speak when the door before her flew open, and a man and woman appeared, light spilling out with them. Their faces were older—more tired—but Mayhap knew them instantly. Her mother's wide-brimmed hat, her long skirt, the freckles beneath her right eye, which were so much like Mayhap's, like specks of splattered coffee. Her father's tweed, his shiny leather shoes, his thick black lashes. Her parents. Her *not*-parents. Their droomhunds sat beside them, peering at Mayhap with knowing eyes.

And behind them stood a girl who looked exactly like her—another Mayhap—with a little black dog of her own.

CHAPTER

Twenty-Seven

The silver grass toyed at Mayhap's back, threading its strands through her hair.

"Ours," it said. "Ours."

Cygnet and Bellwether Ballastian were kneeling beside Pavonine, only a giant's hand away. They were speaking softly, cupping Pavonine's cheeks as she whispered to them. They were taking Winnow's hands and kissing them. Bellwether had one arm around the other Mayhap.

So here Mayhap was, with everything she had ever wanted. Her parents, arrived back. Her parents—*home*. But it was as though she had been given a gift and been made to stand on the other side of a pane of glass, looking at it for all eternity.

She would never sit on her mother's lap. Her mother

would never stroke her hair. She would never even *have* a mother.

Mayhap bit her tongue. She cuddled Seekatrix, burying her face in his scruff.

The Mysteriessa stirred in her chest, where she had always, *always* been—for seven years she had been living there—and Mayhap felt completely wretched.

She heard the click of shoes. She smelled lavender.

The girl who looked exactly like her—the first Mayhap, the *only* Mayhap—peered down at her, holding her droomhund.

The droomhund from the photograph, thought Mayhap. *The girl from the photograph.*

Lit by the moon, the curves of the girl's face were exactly the same as Mayhap's—the slope of her narrow, long nose, the deep bow of her lips. To Mayhap's surprise, the other Mayhap smiled at her. It was an awkward smile but a smile nonetheless. She held out a hand, and Mayhap, still sitting, took it. She said, "Can I tell you a secret?" Mayhap didn't have time to answer before she whispered, "I have always wanted a sister. Especially a sister who looks just like me."

Maybe it was that simple. Maybe she would be a part of this family now, and she would have a new sister. An other-Mayhap. And everything would be fine.

But then the shouting came—Cygnet's stringy cries. "Mayhap Cecily Ballastian! What do you think you are doing?"

Mayhap Cecily Ballastian, Mayhap thought. Of course. That was her name.

Bellwether took other-Mayhap by the elbow and pulled her away, tugging her up the steps. Pavonine stood at her mother's back, and Winnow hovered at her side. Their droomhunds all scuttled behind them, like little shadows with eyes and feet.

Mayhap wanted to break into pieces. Her bones felt as brittle as burned sugar.

The whole family stood together, looking at her.

"I was only trying to be nice," said other-Mayhap.

"You don't know what she's capable of," said Cygnet. "She—"

"What did she do?" asked other-Mayhap.

She doesn't know, thought Mayhap, feeling the Mysteriessa shift in her chest.

"Never you mind, darling," said Cygnet. She crouched and brushed a hand on other-Mayhap's cheek.

"But I want to know," said other-Mayhap softly. "You never tell me anything."

"We don't tell you because it would hurt you," said Bellwether. "Now, go inside and finish your dinner."

153

Other-Mayhap frowned, but she obeyed. She seemed younger than Mayhap, more like Pavonine but less stubborn. Mayhap could see the two sides wrestling within her: the desire to please her parents and the desire to know the truth.

Bellwether trained his eyes on Mayhap. "What are we going to do, Cygnet?" he said. His droomhund scratched at his leg.

Pavonine looked out into the grass with teary eyes.

Winnow was transfixed by the ground.

"She can't stay at the house," said Cygnet. "She's dangerous. Obviously."

"Obviously," said Bellwether.

"We can't leave her out here, though," said Cygnet. "It's cold. And it's dark. She's just a child." She stared into Mayhap's eyes as she said the words, and Mayhap was struck by the sadness in them. "We're going to take you inside," she said, enunciating the words slowly.

"But we can't, Cyg. It's not safe," said Bellwether.

"We can lock her in the upstairs sitting room," said Cygnet. "Until we decide what to do."

Bellwether nodded.

Mayhap wanted to cry out. She wanted to say that she was their family, that she wouldn't hurt anyone, that she hadn't known. But she couldn't form the words.

Winnow was crying.

"You can lock me away," said Mayhap. "But I need to tell you something first. The reason Winnow is sick—it's Evenflee, her droomhund—"

"We know her droomhund's name," said Cygnet bitterly.

"He's trapped inside her mind," said Mayhap. "You need to get him out before—"

Before he scratched away at everything that made Winnow *Winnow*.

Mayhap was afraid that her sister would die if Evenflee stayed there for much longer.

But Cygnet and Bellwether Ballastian only stared at her.

Mayhap swallowed and continued, "I know the Mysteriessa—"

Cygnet stiffened. "You don't *know* her," she said, misunderstanding what Mayhap was about to say. "You *are* her." She looked at Mayhap's breastbone as though she were searching under the fabric of her nightgown for the white-eyed girl. "Don't think I don't know you're in there," she continued, the words vicious. "You have already torn our family apart. Telling us we could find Mayhap if we left and then keeping us from Pavonine and Winnow once we had. The grass wouldn't let us through, no matter how much we fought it." She rolled up the sleeve of her cardigan. There were scars on top of scars on her forearm, as though the grass had burned her skin over and over again. Cygnet's voice cracked. "No. We will deal with this problem on our own. We will find a cure for Winnow on our own." She put a hand on top of Winnow's dark head. Bellwether touched Cygnet's shoulder, clenching his jaw.

Mayhap looked down, ashamed. She wanted to look up. She wanted to deny it. But she carried on staring at her feet. The silver grass swayed around her gently, but it didn't reach out for her. Perhaps even the grass didn't want her anymore.

Cygnet said, "Now, let's go inside." She nodded at Bellwether, putting her arms around Winnow and Pavonine.

Bellwether took Seekatrix away from Mayhap and grabbed her arm.

"No," said Mayhap. "No! You can't take Seeka!"

Bellwether didn't listen. He handed Seekatrix to Cygnet, and she held him fast, even as the droomhund squirmed and cried.

"Pav—" said Mayhap. "Please look after him. Pav—"

Pavonine wouldn't even look at her.

Mayhap kicked and pushed against Bellwether, but she wasn't strong enough to get free.

He dragged her into the house and up the stairs, and Mayhap was so upset that she nearly didn't notice that the house wasn't *her* Straygarden Place but a perfect mirror image of it.

The Mysteriessa sent other-Mayhap here, she thought. *And then Cygnet and Bellwether. A second Straygarden Place.*

Bellwether pushed her through a door and slammed it behind her.

The room—a sitting room with tapestries adorning the walls—was so quiet that all Mayhap could hear was her own breath and Bellwether's receding footsteps.

She had never been so alone before. She had never been locked away before. She had always had Seekatrix by her side. Her heart rattled in her chest with every breath, like an empty bowl, spinning.

She banged on the door. "Let me out!" she called. "Let—me—out!"

But if they heard her, they did not listen.

CHAPTER

Twenty-Eight

They were afraid of her, and so they had locked her away.

Without Seekatrix, Mayhap's heart ached as though it had been trampled. She pressed against her chest with her palm to see if it would ease the pain, but it didn't. She spent some time lying on the floor, staring at the ceiling. She spent some time calling through the keyhole.

Nothing happened. No one came.

After scratching at the door until she had splinters in her fingers and screaming until she was hoarse, Mayhap finally lay down on one of the velvet sofas. The house did not tuck a blanket around her. When she asked it for water, a glass did not appear.

This was *their* house. It was supposed to look after them, not her. Her eyes filled with tears. She missed *her* house. She knew that house. This house was a stranger to her.

Lying still, Mayhap could feel the Mysteriessa against the tender muscle of her heart. She thought that maybe the girl would unfurl—appear to her, talk to her—but she stayed within Mayhap's chest, stubborn as ice on a window.

Mayhap wanted to sleep. She wanted to forget about all of this—who she was and who she wasn't—for only a short while.

But they had taken Seekatrix from her, and so she couldn't.

Unless.

She wasn't a Ballastian—not technically. The Mysteriessa had made her. Maybe she hadn't been robbed of sleep after all. Maybe she'd had the ability to sleep all along.

If she hadn't lost sleep, though, how had the house's magic touched her? She didn't know. But she'd had something else taken from her: a piece of her heart, like a bite out of an apple.

She held her eyes shut, waiting for the white, searing heat to fill the chamber of her mind, bracing for pain.

But it didn't come.

With relief like cashmere, she shut her eyes and let darkness pull her under.

CHAPTER

Twenty-Nine

Mayhap dreamed of a white-haired girl.

The girl walked through a field of silver grass that reached up into the sky.

It wafted around her, brushing her cheeks. It whispered to her.

And it told her stories.

Stories about trees, and birds, and pebbles. Stories about seas, and clouds, and lakes. Stories that ended with princesses. Stories that ended with queens.

"Would Quiverity like to be a queen, like the ones in the stories?" it asked.

Quiverity only ran through the grass, giggling, not taking the question seriously.

But the grass kept asking it, over and over.

"Would Quiverity like to be a queen, like the ones in the stories?"

The girl pushed the grass away and laughed again. Mayhap could see that she did not think of it as a genuine question. She thought it was an affectionate joke. A game she played with the grass, only make-believe.

Eventually, she curled up on the black earth, wet soil kissing her cheek. The grass hung over her like a canopy.

She had slipped halfway into sleep, her eyes closed, the silver covering her like a twilit quilt, when it whispered into her ear.

"Would Quiverity like to be a queen? We would only take something small from her. A small grief, to let the magic in."

Quiverity Edevane nodded her head, and the grass rushed over her like a burial, and even as the silver swallowed her up, still she had the look of someone peaceful, someone loved.

CHAPTER

Thirty

And then Mayhap was awake.

She was so awake that the hairs on her arms were standing to attention.

The house was shaking—the walls trembling like the teeth of shivering children, the little windows cracked and open to the darkness and the drifting wanderroot trees outside. The second Straygarden Place *swayed*.

There was a voice inside Mayhap, and the voice was screaming, "Get out of my house!"

When someone who lives within you screams, it feels as though every one of your veins is a sparking wire. Mayhap curled up and clenched her eyes shut, as though she were trying to hide from lightning.

But the lightning was inside her.

She had to move. She had to speak. She had to tell

the Mysteriessa to calm down. Otherwise she didn't know if she would survive.

She breathed.

And breathed.

And staggered to her feet.

She would speak to the noise within her. To the storm.

She would speak to the Mysteriessa. To the girl named Quiverity Edevane.

Quiverity Edevane, who was shaking the walls and splintering the windows, making the world tilt.

Winnow was not the only one in danger now.

If the house fell, they would all be crushed by the rubble. Faintly, over the howling that came from within her, Mayhap could hear panicked cries.

The Mysteriessa had locked them in. The mother, the father, the sisters—Mayhap could not bring herself to call them *her* sisters anymore. And the droomhunds. *Seekatrix.* Mayhap's heart was sticky as a wound.

Let them try to get out, said the Mysteriessa from the echoing hollow of Mayhap's chest. *Let them try to escape. Let them beg.*

Everything she knew and loved would be destroyed if the Mysteriessa continued like this. The Mysteriessa was powerful enough to do it. To destroy it all. She had magic in her like raging fire, and she'd kept it more or less dampened for seven years, but it was as though someone had stoked it now.

"But why?" Mayhap said. "What made you so angry?"

Then Mayhap remembered the dream. If she had dreamed it, then the Mysteriessa had seen it. And it had made her rage.

They hate me, screamed the Mysteriessa inside her, still from within the cage of Mayhap's bones.

She's hurting, thought Mayhap. *I need to stop this. I need to make her feel better.*

The Mysteriessa had said that you had to hide to be loved, had to trick and fool—that there was no being true and being loved at the same time.

And only Mayhap could prove her wrong.

For Mayhap, in the irony of her living, had been *loved*—unconditionally, fully, lavishly. By her droom-hund. By the girls she had once called her sisters. Her little sister, Pavonine. Her older sister, Winnow.

Before, snarled a breath inside her. *Before Winnow grew curious and went walking in the grass. Before she was led by the silver grass to the house on the other side of the estate. Before she was reunited with her parents. Before she found out what you really were.*

Yes—before Winnow had gone walking in the grass. But there had *been* a before. And that was the point. There had been a time when Mayhap was *loved*.

And she could give that love to the Mysteriessa. She could give Quiverity the belonging she needed, the belonging she had stolen from another family, placed in a little ring box. Maybe that would calm her. Maybe that would prevent her from wrecking the world that Mayhap knew. The world of silver grass and so many windows, of velvet and painted teacups. The world in which her family was alive, in which droomhunds ran along hallways and lived on the dreams of their owners.

Maybe.

She *thought*.

She *hoped*.

She breathed.

And then she spoke.

"Quiverity," she said. "Quiverity, please—there is something I can give you. I didn't see it before, but I do now."

A voice swelled like a rain cloud, within her and without her. *You can give me nothing,* Quiverity told Mayhap.

The ceiling cleaved above Mayhap's head. The curtains whipped past her. Tapestries were yanked off

165

their hooks, dragged across the floor like the trains of dresses. The door to the locked room flew open, ripped from its hinges. It went flying over Mayhap's head and crashed into a wall, falling to the floor.

"Stop!" yelled Mayhap.

But the Mysteriessa only screamed louder. Mayhap curled up on the floor again, covering her head with her arms.

Then she felt fur against her cheek, the wet slick of a tongue.

"Seeka!" she cried. "You found me!"

Seekatrix only looked at her in the silent way that was his habit. She held him fast against her body as though he were a lifebuoy in a jostling sea.

He had been looking for her.

She had not been as alone as she'd thought.

And Quiverity was not alone, either.

But Seekatrix's presence seemed to make Quiverity's anger worse. It shrieked within Mayhap. It gusted and groaned.

Mayhap could not scream louder than the Mysteriessa. She would have to do the opposite. She would have to speak softly.

Silently.

The way Seekatrix spoke to her every day: with the

sort of presence that said *I will never, ever leave you.*

The Mysteriessa was inside her heart, after all. She was a part of her and also *not* a part of her, like peppermint tea in a porcelain cup. Maybe Mayhap could hold a silence so deep that Quiverity would be drawn into it.

Mayhap had never been less certain of anything in her life—but she had to *try.*

Quiverity, she thought, holding the Edevane girl's name in her mind, *I am your family.*

The house stopped shaking. The walls settled like creaking bones.

And the Mysteriessa spoke right into Mayhap's heart.

I am not worthy of family, she said. *You insult me by saying otherwise.*

She lifted a cry so devastating that Mayhap was sure the entire house had gone up in flames. Mayhap closed her eyes. But when she opened them again, Seekatrix was still pressed against her chest, and the house was still standing.

The blaze had been in her.

The room was still.

She spoke again, this time with the tongue the Mysteriessa had fashioned: "Quiverity—the grass *tricked* you. It got you to agree to something you never would have agreed to if you'd known—"

"I did know! I *had* to know! I knew what would happen, and I accepted anyway."

"You didn't," Mayhap said quietly. "I know you didn't. I saw you—I saw you in my dream. Quiverity, you made me so that you could have your family back. You loved them. You wouldn't so easily have given them up. You said yourself—you were half-asleep when the grass asked you. You loved us. Tutto—all that time, all those stories he read to Pavonine, how kind he was. That was you. You made him come alive. For us."

The Mysteriessa's rage cooled within Mayhap.

"I am your home. Your family," continued Mayhap aloud. "I am here for you. I *love* you."

The Mysteriessa wept, and Mayhap did the same, crying into Seekatrix's fur.

"You can't take back the past," said Mayhap. "But you can decide what you want today to be like."

"But they hate me," said the Mysteriessa. "They have always hated me—"

"You took their sister—their daughter—away," said Mayhap. "I know you gave them *me* to replace her, but—"

"I kept her safe. I made a second Straygarden Place only for her, a house that would always look after her. Her parents wanted to fetch her back. But I couldn't let them. I only wanted to belong—to belong to something, to someone. I loved the Ballastians. I really loved them. And Winnow—I never meant for her to get so sick. I only wanted her to stay asleep. To keep my secret. I didn't know it would all go so horribly wrong."

Mayhap spoke as though her words were being chiseled into stone. "I know," she said. "I know. And you *do* belong to someone. You belong to me. *With* me."

The windows began to rattle again, a crystalline crescendo. And then they all shattered at once, each a leaf in a forest of glass. The walls shattered, too. The floors. The ceilings.

In a moment, the second Straygarden Place turned to dust.

And Mayhap was thrown into the cold night air.

CHAPTER
Thirty-One

The grass caught Mayhap gently, handling her as a girl would handle a moth's lost wing.

When she opened her eyes, she was surrounded by silver. Seekatrix was still against her chest. Her heart danced, and she felt the droomhund's smaller heart dancing, too.

Bright white stars burned their patterns into the black sheet of the sky. Wanderroot trees drifted past. The grass hoisted her higher so that she could see the clearing where the second Straygarden Place had once been.

It was gone.

Every tapestry, every chair, every carpet, every painting. All of it had turned to dust, and that dust hung around Mayhap like starlight. She turned her head to see that the first Straygarden Place still stood. It looked small, like a dollhouse.

Mayhap couldn't see her family in the grass. Her stomach was a nest of withered branches.

She had made a terrible mistake.

And now everything had been destroyed.

"Pavonine?" she said. "Winnow?"

Seekatrix stirred in her arms.

And the Mysteriessa spoke.

She spoke the way rain falling on moss would speak, soaking Mayhap through. It was like diving into a river headfirst, like stepping into a field of silver grass and letting it sway over you, filtering the evening's dusk.

Whatever that voice was, she was beneath it, under it, in it. She *was* it.

Did you really mean it? said the Mysteriessa. *Did you really mean it when you said that I—that I belonged to you?*

Mayhap took a breath. "Yes, I did," she answered.

It was no lie. She had been made by this girl. She belonged to Quiverity the way a garden belongs to the sun. And that meant that Quiverity belonged to her, too. For good. For bad.

The grass settled her on her feet, and something in Mayhap relaxed, a ribbon unwound. But she could not stop thinking of her family. "Are they safe?" she asked.

"They're safe," said Quiverity Edevane, appearing beside Mayhap. "They're in the grass. Let me show you."

CHAPTER
Thirty-Two

Mayhap and Quiverity found the Ballastian family—mother, father, three sisters, and five droomhunds—in a space the grass had made for them. It looked like a silver cave.

Before, the grass had been eager to grab hold of Mayhap, to twist about her arms and legs. But now it stood apart from her—apart from all of them—as though it were watching. Waiting.

Mayhap's skin prickled. She didn't know what the grass was waiting for, but while it stood still, she could try to make Winnow better.

She could try to save her sister.

Winnow was lying in the center of the clearing, the grass making moonshadows on her skin. She looked like a sculpture. All the words Mayhap couldn't say caught in her throat like barbed hooks. She wanted to say her sister's name—she *was* her sister, she *was*—but she couldn't.

The Ballastians were standing around Winnow, bowing their heads.

Bellwether was speaking very quickly: "I don't understand. It should have worked. After all our research on the subject—"

Cygnet squeezed his shoulder. "Bell," she said. "I don't think there's anything else we can do." Her face was as white as a winter moon. "We've—lost her."

Her droomhund whined.

"We can't have lost her," said Bellwether.

"But we have," said Cygnet, leaning over to place a cheek against Winnow's. "She's not breathing. She has no pulse."

Tears were dripping off Pavonine's chin as she looked at the dirt beneath her feet.

It was other-Mayhap who spotted Mayhap and the Mysteriessa.

"Mamma," she said, pulling at Cygnet's sleeve. "Mamma, the other Mayhap is here."

Cygnet turned her head to see Mayhap and Quiverity standing hand in hand, their backs to the grass that framed the silver cave. She moved to stand between them and Winnow. Other-Mayhap and Pavonine stayed where they were. Other-Mayhap whispered, "Who's that?" and pointed at the Mysteriessa. Pavonine said, "Shhh." Bellwether stiffened.

The grass began to whisper.

"Ours, ours, ours."

"You can't have her," said Bellwether.

"I've come to help," said Mayhap. "I *know* what's wrong with her. I know what will make her better. Please. Let us try. Otherwise we really will lose her. You will lose her."

On her bed of dark earth, in her green coat, Winnow looked like a princess, her hair blown away from her face by the breeze rushing through the grass, her skin as shiny as mercury.

"Mamma," said other-Mayhap. "You've been looking for my sisters for so long, hurting yourself for it. Now that they're finally here, you won't let Winnow die, will you?" There were tears in her eyes.

Pavonine spoke now, looking at the toes of her boots. "Mayhap was my sister for seven years—seven years and she was never anything but good to me. She has—I think she has—a good heart."

Cygnet and Bellwether considered their daughters' words. They looked at Pavonine, then at other-Mayhap, and then at Winnow. This was probably, in the end, what made them agree to it: the fact that they had no other hope.

Only Mayhap could help.

Only the Mysteriessa could make Winnow better.

And so Cygnet and Bellwether stepped apart, allowing Mayhap and Quiverity to come closer.

Mayhap kneeled at Winnow's side. She squeezed her silver hand. It was a relief for Winnow not to flinch at her touch. She knew that once Winnow woke, she probably wouldn't ever want to see her again. It hurt. But it hurt her more to see her sister suffering. She looked at the Mysteriessa. "I think you know what to do," she said.

Quiverity Edevane gave a curt nod.

She sank to her knees and placed a hand over Winnow's ear. She held it there.

Cygnet hid her face, crying out. Bellwether stared at the Mysteriessa's hand with horror on his face. Other-Mayhap was wearing her awkward smile, and Pavonine's eyes were shiny.

And then Quiverity drew Evenflee—a scraggly mess of black fur, wriggling like a new puppy—from Winnow's mind. The dog squirmed and cried, pushing his body against the Mysteriessa's chest and panting.

Cygnet and Bellwether seemed to be holding their

breath, staring at Winnow. Pavonine ran to sit by Mayhap's side and took her hand and held it. Other-Mayhap breathed in: an exclamation of wonder. The Mysteriessa breathed out, as though relieved it was finally, finally, over.

And Winnow opened her eyes.

CHAPTER

Thirty-Three

The silver began to recede from Winnow's skin.

Cygnet and Bellwether gathered closer to watch, their droomhunds sniffing Winnow's fingertips. Pavonine's mouth was open. Other-Mayhap came close, too, patting Evenflee, who was still in the Mysteriessa's arms.

The silver drew itself away from Winnow like mist lifting away from a lake. Her skin, inch by inch, was restored to its creamy tone. The silver was drawn out of her eyes, too, until they returned to their usual richness—so dark you could hardly see her pupils. She blinked, trying to focus on the faces that peered down at her.

She wriggled her fingers, her toes. She sat up, ever so slowly, as though she were afraid the silver would come for her again.

Pavonine let go of Mayhap's hand and launched herself at Winnow, tumbling on top of her. "Winn," she said. "You're here. You're better."

Winnow ran a hand over Pavonine's head. "I'm better," she said.

"I missed you," said Pavonine, resting her head on Winnow's shoulder.

Peffiandra jumped up to lick Winnow's cheeks.

Cygnet and Bellwether quietly reached down to take Winnow's hands in theirs.

Other-Mayhap stood behind her parents.

Then Winnow's eyes found Mayhap's face—and Quiverity's. Her body jerked.

The Mysteriessa put Evenflee down gently. The droomhund ran to Winnow as Quiverity stood and drifted toward the silver grass.

There seemed so much to say, but Mayhap couldn't find a way to say it.

She wanted to say *I love you.*

She wanted to say *I'm sorry.*

She wanted to say *I didn't know. I didn't know all the wrong I had done.*

But she couldn't. The air was too gentle for it. The world felt like a bruise. She didn't want to hurt it further.

Instead, she turned to Quiverity Edevane, her sister through all of this, and she said, "Maybe we should go."

Go *where,* she didn't know, but this clearing was for the Ballastians. They had righted their wrong, and they could not stay.

Quiverity only looked at Mayhap, but her eyes said, *I am afraid, but I will come with you.*

Mayhap stood. She picked Seekatrix up. "Goodbye," she said.

But Pavonine whined. "Tell her," she said to Mayhap. "Tell Winnow what happened."

Winnow frowned at Pavonine, one arm around her, then glanced at Mayhap.

Other-Mayhap looked as though she were about to hear the greatest bedtime story ever told.

Mayhap cleared her throat. She couldn't bring herself to lift her eyes from the soil. "I didn't know," she said as loudly as she could muster. "I didn't know who—*what*—I was. I didn't know that Quiverity—the Mysteriessa—made me seven years ago. She made me to steal *her* place." Mayhap motioned at other-Mayhap. "When I found out how she had made you sick, I tried to help. Anyway, I am glad you are well now, Winnow." The wind whistled around them. "She did it because she was afraid, because she knew you'd found out that I wasn't—that I wasn't your sister."

"I was afraid, too. I was afraid for Pavonine," said Winnow, bursting into tears. "I came back to get her. I was going to tell her once you were asleep. I was going to take her away. To Mamma and Pappa. To the second house. The grass wouldn't let them through, but it would let me. It let me come back to the first Straygarden Place. But then it all went wrong."

"I understand," said Mayhap. "It wasn't right, what the Mysteriessa did. And now I think we must go. So that you can start over."

Winnow fiddled with her cuff.

Pavonine ran to Mayhap and hugged her.

Mayhap took her time, looking at their faces. She did not know where she would go or what she would find when she arrived elsewhere, but she knew that she would always remember them.

Pavonine let go of Mayhap's waist and squeezed her hand. Cygnet and Bellwether were huddled together, turning their faces away, and other-Mayhap was watching all of this with wide eyes, holding her droomhund like a baby.

Mayhap freed her hand from Pavonine's. She walked

to the edge of the clearing, the Mysteriessa at her side.

The grass hissed, as though waking up.

"Where are you going?" it said.

And it curled around Mayhap's wrists.

CHAPTER

Thirty-Four

The grass wound Mayhap up in silver. It wrapped itself around Winnow, Pavonine, and other-Mayhap. It held Cygnet and Bellwether still as they struggled against its tangling. Mayhap could hear them shouting, but she couldn't make out the words. The droomhunds were trapped, too, whining and barking.

The only one the grass had left alone was Quiverity Edevane.

The earth at Mayhap's feet grew soggy, and she was sucked into it. Her sisters and other-Mayhap were slurped down, too.

"What's happening?" she heard Winnow say. "Is it the Mysteriessa again?"

"No," said Mayhap. "It's the grass."

The Mysteriessa couldn't help them. The grass had given her magic, but it was far more powerful than she was.

The sisters and almost-sisters were pulled down into the earth. Into the darkness of the mud. Into the glut of soil.

Mayhap tried to cry out and tasted the saltiness of clay, the squirm of worms, the grit of crushed, chalky stone. She tasted centuries.

Strands of grass cut into her wrists, her middle, her ankles. Her nose and mouth and ears were clogged, and she thrashed and twisted, needing to breathe.

Just when she thought she could not live without air for another second, she began to fall.

She could breathe—a gasp, only one—before she landed on the ground below her with a thud. Her hands went to her ears and nose and throat, but her skin was dry and dirtless. Her ears rang like bells. She moved, loosed from her silver bonds.

Her sisters fell, too.

"Pav?" she called. "Winnow?" In the dark, her mouth was scoured by their names.

"I'm here," said Pavonine.

"Me, too," said Winnow.

"I think the grass left Mamma and Pappa—and the droomhunds—up there," said other-Mayhap.

"What's happening?" said Winnow.

"I don't know," said Mayhap.

"Shhh," said Pavonine. "Can you hear that?"

"Hear what?" said Winnow.

"That," said other-Mayhap.

"It's—it sounds like grass," said Pavonine.

It *did* sound like grass. Rustling.

"Who's there?" said Mayhap, her voice in the key of fear.

"Shhh," said Pavonine, loudly now, for the grass's sound had risen around them like a wave, and it seemed about to respond.

Then something else happened. *Light* happened. Bright, white light, as though the earth had been opened like a pomegranate. The ground they had fallen through was now turning itself inside out—turning itself so that its silver grass hung low over them, a canopy of shining threads, sharp as needles. The earth above them flipped over and shut itself like the lid of a pot, and light shone through fissures above.

"Please," said Mayhap, choking on the smell of the soil. "Don't hurt us."

"Friends of Quiverity Edevane, are you?" said the grass.

Mayhap squirmed as the silver brushed her skin. "Y-yes," she stuttered. "We are."

"That's not exactly—" began Winnow.

"Hush," said Pavonine.

Other-Mayhap stayed quiet.

The grass laughed. Its laugh was like paper cuts against Mayhap's skin—the sharp edge of something delicate. "Quiverity Edevane," it mused. "But she has not a friend in the world. She has told us herself. Why else would she steal one Mayhap away and replace her with another? A girl like a trap. A hole in her heart big enough for a rat."

Mayhap struggled to breathe, the air around her warm and thick, the grass chiming at her cheeks. "She was lonely," she said. "But now she has us."

"Not *us*," came Winnow's voice.

Pavonine cleared her throat.

Other-Mayhap didn't make a sound.

"Fine," said Mayhap. "Now she has *me*."

"You think you can be sisters after this. After all of this. That is wishful, little wishful one," said the grass.

All the while, as the grass was speaking, Mayhap was trying to put all the pieces of the puzzle together.

Think of an animal, think of a place. Think of a person, think of a face.

Straygarden Place. Quiverity Edevane. The silver grass.

Think of an animal, think of a place. Think of a person, think of a face.

"Wishful one?" she said. "But you are the one who is wishful."

"We do not *wish*!" said the grass. "We have the most magic in all of this barren place. We do not wish. We do. We make. We—*are*."

Mayhap knew that she had touched on something true, because the grass's words thrummed with anger, with hurt, with—*longing*.

She thought about the wanderroot trees, the silver grass pressing itself against glass—looking in, always looking in. She thought about the windows, opened and squealing on their hinges like out-of-tune violins. She thought about the bats in the conservatory, quivering among branches. She thought about the dead plants, too, and her parents' work—trying to determine why nothing grew at Straygarden Place except silver grass and floating trees.

"There is one thing you cannot do," said Mayhap, folding her arms and planting her feet.

"Mayhap," said Winnow, "don't anger it."

"Shhh," said Pavonine.

Other-Mayhap held her tongue.

"We too would like to hear what we cannot do," laughed the grass, its strands parting.

Mayhap steeled herself, digging her heels into the bedrock below her. She thought of Quiverity Edevane losing her family. It hadn't made sense to Mayhap before, but now it did. Now *all* of it did. It all clicked like keys in locks, turning with the thrill of metal unhooking metal.

"Quiverity told me that you can't give your magic away," she said, louder than her heart cared for, "unless someone has a crack in them."

"We can do anything we want!" shrieked the grass. It wound its silver around her again, hugging her tighter and tighter.

"That's why you killed Quiverity's family," said Mayhap. "She needed a crack in her, didn't she? And you had to make it."

"And why would we, great as we are, want to give away our magic—our power?" The grass's many voices were angry now, multiplying like bats in a night sky, bright as stars and sharp as diamonds.

But it didn't tighten further around Mayhap. It wanted her to answer. It wanted her to speak.

"Because," she said, "you have so much magic that nothing can grow around you. You have so much magic that you are alone. No one wants to be alone. Not me, not Quiverity. Not even you. The cost of light is darkness. And the cost of magic is loneliness. You press your silver against the windows because you are lonely. You steal bats because you are lonely. You watch us because you want to be like us. You want what we have. You want what Quiverity wanted. A family."

The grass stopped rustling. It loosened its grip on Mayhap, and in the dim light she could see the whip-like twines around her, spitting and sparking. "It is the truth the girl speaks," said the grass. "It is our one defeat."

Relief like a storm-flooded river.

Until the grass spoke again.

"But you, Mayhap, will help us."

Mayhap's breath was punched out of her lungs. "What?" She fumbled for words. "But I—I won't accept it. I won't accept your magic."

"It's not *you* we want to offer it to," said the grass. "It is Quiverity Edevane. It is time we gave her *more* magic. Last time, the rift we opened in her could have swallowed a minor sea, and she took only some. But if we take *you* from her—a girl she made, a girl who loves her unconditionally despite what she did, despite who she is—she will split wide enough for *all* of it.

For *all* of our magic. That is why we need you. That is why we whispered to Winnow. That is why we set her roaming, led her to the other Straygarden Place. So that Quiverity could lose you. So that we could kill you, now that you have known her and loved her."

Pavonine began to sob loudly.

"Please," Mayhap said. She had no more plans and no more schemes. "Please, don't do this. You don't want to give away *all* your magic, do you?"

The grass seemed to really think about the prospect. "We do," it said at long last. "The cost of magic is too grave. We were an ordinary field of grass until a golden feather fell from the sky and made us what we are. But then there was too much magic in us and nothing green could grow beside us. Our magic overwhelmed even the sturdiest plant. We made the floating trees—the ones your mother named *wanderroot*. We watched their flowers blooming above us. But we want roots beside us. We want a tree, a thorny flower. We want a bird singing on a branch."

"I'm sorry," said Mayhap. "Loneliness is as bad as any other sickness."

The grass only laughed. "We won't be lonely anymore—not after this."

And it began to tighten around Mayhap again.

Tighter and tighter.

"Goodbye, Mayhap," it said.

"No!" screamed Pavonine.

"No," whimpered Winnow.

The world sputtered out of view.

Then other-Mayhap spoke: "Wait! You don't have to do this! Give it to *us*!"

The grass loosened—just enough for Mayhap's vision to clear.

"Give it to the four of us," said other-Mayhap. "We will accept it gladly. The Mysteriessa already has so much of your power—she might not survive receiving the rest. But *we* could take it. We've never had magic before, so we could take plenty. We could divide it between us. Please."

The grass was silent for a long time. Then it said, "But you must have a rift in you. A crack where the magic can slip in, like moonlight through a slightly open window."

"Yes," said other-Mayhap. "But we have already lost so much. You wouldn't even have to make the crack. Take a look."

Winnow and Pavonine exchanged a glance.

The grass was silent again, as though perplexed. But it let go of Mayhap, and then she could feel cold sifting through her, and she knew that the grass was searching her for the cracks that other-Mayhap had spoken of. Her sisters were doubled over. The grass was searching through them, too.

"Ah," said the grass. "The girl is right." Its tendrils rushed and rustled like a contented sigh. "These four are like dolls fallen from a shelf. One Mayhap, who knows she was made for evil—made with a hole in her heart for a lonely girl to creep into. And another Mayhap, who was separated from her sisters at the age of only five. And Pavonine, who lost her parents when she was a baby. And Winnow—why, Winnow was attacked, her droomhund made into a weapon, her sister into an enemy. They all have cracks in them, cracks our magic can seep into."

The sisters of Straygarden Place—all four of them— held their breath.

The grass wavered. It seemed to be thinking things over. Then, finally, it said, "Four girls to tuck the magic into—that's better than one."

"Do we have a deal?" asked other-Mayhap. "We agree to take your magic. But you must promise not to hurt this Mayhap or the white-eyed girl. Or anyone."

The grass hummed. "We have already forgotten about killing now that we do not need to anymore."

"All right," said other-Mayhap.

She took Pavonine's hand, and Pavonine reached for Mayhap's. Winnow took other-Mayhap's hand, too, and together they filled their lungs, ready to receive the magic that the grass so desperately wanted to give away.

"We will take it," said other-Mayhap. "We will take it together."

"We will take it together," said Pavonine.

"We will take it together," said Winnow.

"We will take it together," said Mayhap.

CHAPTER

Thirty-Five

The magic felt like someone singing, very loudly, in Mayhap's ears. It felt like being drenched in something teeth-clatteringly cold.

She was sugar dissolving in tea.

She was sunlight through a window.

She was a still, clear pond.

She was sky, star-shatters, a hungry darkness.

All her broken places closed up, scabs over wounds. But as the magic pushed its way into her brain—her heart, her gut—they opened again.

And she understood: you needed a crack in you because the magic required space to slip *inside,* but also because it had to have a way to slip *out*—to touch the world.

CHAPTER

Thirty-Six

The grass was right way up again.

The silver grass, which had once been so tall—taller than mansions—had lost its shine. It was simply gray now, gray as a rainy day's sky, and short, too—only as high as a girl's ankle.

Mayhap stretched out her arm to run her fingers through it, grabbing a tuft. She squeezed it, tore the blades out of the ground. They lay limp in her fist.

Winnow's dark hair resolved before her, a silver streak among the curls like a river in a mountainside. Then Mayhap saw Pavonine's pout, and the sleeve of other-Mayhap's coat. The droomhunds were little mounds of blackest fur. The whole world had separated itself into shifting blocks, and now it all shifted back, slowly, into proper position. A finished puzzle.

There was Winnow—whole. And Pavonine, too. And other-Mayhap. They were lying on their sides in the grass. And there were Seekatrix, and Peffiandra, and Evenflee, and other-Mayhap's droomhund. They were wagging their tails.

There they were. There they all were.

And it was morning, somehow.

Mayhap held Seekatrix and closed her eyes.

She did not know what it meant to have magic. But there was one person who could tell her.

"Quiverity?" she called out. She walked over the gray grass, crunching it beneath her feet.

She walked until she could see the first Straygarden Place. It was so far away that it looked only about the size of a hand. The wanderroot trees were sprawled across the now-ordinary field, unfloating, lying in heaps, their branches broken, their flowers crushed. The white bats that had been shaken from their branches dove through the sky in confused patterns. Seekatrix whimpered.

"Quiverity!" Mayhap called.

And found the girl standing right behind her.

"You don't need me anymore," Quiverity said.

"Of course I do," said Mayhap. "We're family. We are. You are my sister."

"I'm not your sister," said Quiverity sadly.

"You were a part of me for all my life. You are still."

Quiverity's mouth crumpled. "I'm sorry I let the grass get you."

"The grass killed your family. It took everything from you." Mayhap looked around her. "Are you still afraid of it?" she asked.

Quiverity didn't answer, only shuffled her feet on the ground.

Mayhap held Quiverity's fears in her hands as carefully as she would've held a newborn bat pup, and Quiverity did the same for Mayhap. And there, between them, all was forgiven.

In the distance, Cygnet hugged other-Mayhap and Pavonine. Bellwether crouched beside Winnow. They were checking to see if they were all right—their real daughters. Mayhap ached, but the feeling was more like love than loss.

She wiped her tears away. "We still have a house," she said to Quiverity. "We could return there. To the first Straygarden Place."

Quiverity fixed her gaze on the mansion. "I think it is time for me to leave this place," she said. "I think—I think I would like to leave."

"Then I will come with you," said Mayhap.

When they looked at the horizon, it seemed like a path to a new place.

The Ballastians could stay here, could continue living at Straygarden Place, but Mayhap and Quiverity couldn't. It wasn't theirs anymore.

And so they left the Ballastians behind, for Cygnet and Bellwether were caring for their own, and the two girls—one with coffee-freckles and one with white, white eyes—didn't want to disturb that sort of love, the sort that tends to wounds.

CHAPTER

Thirty-Seven

Quiverity, Mayhap, and Seekatrix walked toward the wrought iron gate that Mayhap had seen in the contract's dream.

Silence buzzed between them like insects.

Mayhap's name broke it.

"Mayhap!" called Winnow.

Other voices joined in, like a handful of picked flowers.

Fear twisted Quiverity's lips.

"Don't worry," Mayhap whispered. She turned around to see three girls with dark, streaming hair running toward her, their droomhunds sprinting alongside them.

Winnow, Pavonine, and other-Mayhap tumbled before her, laughing, their mouths full of morning air. They all had silver streaks in their hair now.

Winnow said, "Where are you going?" through labored breaths, and Pavonine jumped up and clung to Mayhap's shoulders.

"We're leaving," said Mayhap.

"You can't go!" said other-Mayhap. "We don't want you to go."

"We want you to stay," said Pavonine. Peffiandra sat beside her and barked once.

"We're bound now—by magic," said Winnow. She eyed Quiverity carefully, then closed her hands as if she were holding a butterfly. When she opened them again, a tiny black puppy squirmed in her palms. She stepped toward Quiverity, handing it to her. "Now you can have your own droomhund," she said.

Quiverity held the puppy gently, stroking its head with one finger.

"We'd like you to stay, too," Winnow told Quiverity.

"Are you sure?" said the girl with white eyes. "I almost—"

"But you didn't," said Winnow, cutting her off. "And you saved me in the end. I don't know about you, but it's the endings of stories that matter to me, not so much the beginnings. And people are like stories if you give them enough time to reveal themselves."

"What about your parents?" said Quiverity. "What will they say?"

Cygnet and Bellwether Ballastian were standing in the distance, their arms around each other. Their droomhunds sat beside them, watchful.

"They want to continue their work," said other-Mayhap. "On magic and the natural world."

Pavonine said, "They're not only *our* parents. They're yours, too."

Cygnet waved. Her face held an expression that was at once pained and hopeful.

Seekatrix scratched at Quiverity's leg, sniffing the air for the puppy's scent. The other dogs howled melodiously.

"You've been alone for a long time, Quiv," said Mayhap. "But you don't have to be alone anymore. We could stay if you like."

"Yes," said Quiverity Edevane, so softly it seemed only the sky would hear her—only the bats diving for their last dragonflies and their last fruit.

But it didn't matter.

Her sisters had heard her.

Her sisters had heard her, and that was enough.

ACKNOWLEDGMENTS

I'd like to thank Patricia Nelson for all the exclamation marks and good advice, and for encouraging even my strangest ideas. I wouldn't be able to do any of this without you. Miriam Newman, for loving the Ballastian sisters as much as I do. Thank you for getting it. Thank you for helping me to get there. Emma Lidbury, for giving *Straygarden* a home in the UK. Pam Consolazio, for all the beautiful grass and the last-minute cover magic! The copyeditors, Betsy Uhrig and Jackie Houton, for knowing things I didn't. The proofreaders, Matt Seccombe and Julia Gaviria, for noticing things I couldn't. Erin Farley, Rita Csizmadia, and Angie Dombroski: thank you, thank you, thank you.

To everyone at Candlewick Press and Walker Books UK: thank you for giving this story a home. Thank you for helping to turn it into an Actual, Real Book. This still feels like a miracle to me, and it probably always will. I'm so honored to be a part of the Candlewick and Walker family.

I also have to mention Kris Reynolds, who reads messy drafts and cheers me on; Rachael Romero, who believes in magic as much as I do; Lindsay Eagar, who gives me the space to be ambitious; Alison Lowry, who told me to keep going; and Kate Rogan at Love Books, who has always supported my writing.

To the librarians and teachers who have invited me into their libraries and classrooms, and to the young readers who ask questions about my stories: thank you. You remind me why I write.

I feel so deeply grateful for my family: Daddy, for believing in me unfailingly. Mama, for teaching me to notice things. Chalk, for challenging me and listening to me. You are my daily inspiration. Ash, for being my wonderful baby sister. Tam, for walking a path ahead of me. Tatum, for arriving on the eighth of December. Darfer, for being the very first droomhund. All the other magical dogs in the Chewins clan—especially Kimchi, Soju, Rosie, and Favey, who helped to inspire Evenflee, Seekatrix, and Peffiandra. And finally: Liale, my favorite person and forever-crush. Thank you for truly seeing me, for joy and adventures, and for never once saying *maybe not*. I love you.